MAGIC AND MAYHEM

The Raven Mysteries

Also by Marcus Sedgwick
for older readers

Blood Red, Snow White
The Book of Dead Days
The Dark Flight Down
The Dark Horse
Floodland
The Foreshadowing
The Kiss of Death
Revolver
My Swordhand is Singing
White Crow
Witch Hill

The Raven Mysteries

Flood and Fang
Ghosts and Gadgets
Lunatics and Luck
Vampires and Volts

For more information visit –

www.marcussedgwick.com

www.ravenmysteries.co.uk

MAGIC AND MAYHEM

The Raven Mysteries

Book 5

MARCUS SEDGWICK

Illustrated by Pete Williamson

Orion
Children's Books

First published in Great Britain in 2011
by Orion Children's Books
a division of the Orion Publishing Group Ltd
Orion House
5 Upper St Martin's Lane
London WC2H 9EA
A Hachette UK Company

1 3 5 7 9 10 8 6 4 2

A catalogue record for this book is available from
the British Library.

ISBN 978 1 84255 697 9

Printed in Great Britain by
CPI Mackays, Chatham ME5 8TD

www.orionbooks.co.uk

For bunnies everywhere

Otherhand

One

Castle Otherhand
is home to
all sorts of
oddballs, lunatics
and fruitcakes.
It's just as well
for all of them
that they have
a secret weapon:
he's called Edgar.

A bored bird is a dangerous bird.

That's what my dear old ma used to say when I was a young ravenlet: a bored bird is a dangerous bird. A naughty bird. Even perhaps a little bit of an evil bird.

In fact, throughout history, when ravens have taken the blame for badness, I'll bet you a sack of mice it was a bored bird that caused the trouble.

Let me tell you a tale of the trouble that happened in Castle Otherhand just a little while ago; a whole heap of trouble, more irritating than a monkey with a trumpet. A whole heap of trouble, I say, none of which would have happened if I hadn't been so brain-meltingly bored.

It went like this.

Nothing much had happened in Castle Otherhand
for really quite some time. After that business
with the fang-toothed beastie in the cellars,
and the commotion with ghosts, and then the
blood-curdling episode with the undead, there
had been a long spell, of well . . . nothing.

Now to start with, I was all in favour of
a bit of peace and quiet. It allowed me to get on
with some uninterrupted sulking, for one thing.
I spent a few weeks counting how many of my
feathers had gone grey, and then another few
weeks double-checking the answer.

I passed happy days gliding round the
valley, enjoying simply being a big black bird

with a shiny black beak; that was
enough for me.

But then, something
strange happened to me.

It started one morning as a tiny tickle in
my brain box, and though I tried to ignore it, I
couldn't. It grew.

And by the end of the day, I had to
admit it.

I was bored.

And not just a little bit bored, but so
bored I would have pecked my own head if such
a thing were possible.

Instead I started to peck at the wallpaper
in the Red Room with such fury and intent that
Solstice heard me from along the corridor and

came to investigate.

'Edgar,' she said gently. 'Are you normal?'

That's rich coming from an Otherhand. Normal doesn't even enter into it.

I decided not to answer her, but kept on banging my beak on the wall, until I'd made a tidy hole, just right for hiding a dried mouse in. In case of emergency, you know.

'Really, Edgar,' cooed Solstice, 'I do think it might be best to stop doing that. Really I do.'

Well, that was enough for me. Red rag to

a bull. Monkey's bottom to a swiftly-aimed kick.

I pecked with renewed
vigour, and was pleased to
note that a couple of paintings
fell off the wall. At full pelt,
I could give a woodpecker a
run for his money.

'I think perhaps you're
not feeling terribly well. Is that it, Edgar dear?'

I was now firmly stuck on peck-o-matic,
but dimly aware that Solstice had a point. Of sorts.

Because no, I was not ill. What I was, was
B. O. R. E. D.

I knew there and then that if something
exciting, possibly scary, and maybe even perhaps
outright life-threatening did not occur in the castle

very soon, I would lose total grip on my marbles.

So I decided to make something happen, and the way I did it was pretty cunning, let me tell you.

I spent the next day and a half zooming round the castle like a guided missile, pecking anyone and everyone on the head repeatedly until I was in too great a danger of being swiped at. I would then proceed to my next victim, and so forth and so on, until pretty much everyone in the place was going spare.

Cudweed summed it up as I buried my beak into his blasted monkey yet again.

'Mother!' he cried. 'Edgar's gone funny in the head.'

Ha! I thought. Ha!

And then I overdid it.

I spied Lord Valevine and Flinch heading to the laboratory in the East Tower. Valevine had been working on some invention or other for days, and although I didn't know exactly what it was, I knew he was getting very steamed up about the whole thing.

As I burst into the lab, he was explaining something to Flinch.

'If we don't get this cabbage-counting machine working, Flinch, and this very afternoon, I swear I shall not be held responsible for my actions! Who would have thought it was this hard? I . . .'

I heard no more of Valevine's moaning, because I chose that moment to set about him, face and neck.

Well, that was it.

I think it's fair to say that I had overdone it, and within half an hour I found myself locked in my bird cage in the Red Room, with the whole family standing around it, looking exasperated.

And cross.

'What are we going to do with him?' Minty asked.

'If I had my way ...' Valevine began, but Solstice interrupted.

'But fortunately you've been outvoted, Father,' she said. 'I think we need to understand

raven psychology . . .'

'You mean what's going on in the bird

brain?' Cudweed asked.

If I had eyebrows I would have used them to good purpose at this point.

'Well, sort of,' Solstice said. 'I simply mean that we need to understand what is going on in poor Edgar's head. That's all.'

'**Ark!**' I shrieked.

'There! You see!'

'Well, good luck with that, daughter of mine,' Valevine said. 'I've been trying to work that out since I was a boy, with no success, whatsoever. But I tell you, if this behaviour goes on, he's in big trouble, and never mind whether I was outvoted.'

Valevine looked so thunderously cross that I was almost scared. Almost.

Solstice looked nervous.

'I have an idea,' she said. 'Perhaps we should get out of the castle for a short while, and leave Father to his own devices. I saw a poster for a circus, down in the valley. Maybe we should all have a nice day trip?'

'Oh, yes!' cried Cudweed.

'Capital idea!' exclaimed Valevine. 'The lot of you can clear off and give me some room for the massive exertion of my brain!'

'Yes, very good idea, dear,' said Minty.

So we went to the circus, and that was to be the start of it all.

The magic.

And the mayhem.

Two

Every midsummer's eve the Otherhands hold a massive party in the woods above the lake, with music, dancing, and fireworks at midnight.

What more innocent thing could there be than to take a trip to the circus? Only the Otherhand family could turn it into an international incident.

I probably wasn't helping matters. I'd calmed down a bit after my earlier frenzy, but I thought I'd make sure no one had forgotten how bored I was by giving anything that moved an encouraging stab of the beak now and again.

Cudweed was hunting for Fellah, and was blaming me for his disappearance, claiming I'd pecked him beyond the point a monkey could bear.

Solstice was panicking about what a fashion-conscious teen Goth should wear to the circus, and Minty was having a row with Valevine about why there was another huge delivery of cabbages in the Small Hall.

Fizz and Buzz had been placed in a large buggy on at least three occasions, but kept climbing out when no one was looking,

Grandma Slivinkov was doggedly pursuing one of them, and it might have been Fizz and it might have been Buzz, as the tiny terror crawled inside the head of a large tigerskin rug.

'It's so my machine has something to count,' Lord Otherhand explained, his patience tested to the limit. 'Without cabbages, there wouldn't be much point in a cabbage-counting machine, would there?'

'But why do we need a cabbage-counting machine at all?' Minty cried, nearly at her wits' end. She was trying to pull on a long pair of boots, getting ready to take everyone to the circus.

Valevine rolled his eyes and then addressed his wife as if he was speaking to a dim-witted penguin.

'Well, I would have thought that was obvious,' he said. He gestured to the vast pile of greenage mounting up in the Hall. 'That lot are simply not going to count themselves, are they? Eh?'

He spun on his heel, triumphant.

Minty stared at his back, open-mouthed, and then said in a very quiet voice, 'Right. That's it. Everyone out of the castle now, before I murder my husband.'

There was something about her tone that had everyone outside and trolling down the driveway in under ninety seconds.

It was a rather lovely day. Birds of a small size were chirping in the trees as our jolly band passed by. I glared at them, just to make sure they knew who was boss, but I didn't really mean it. I was already feeling much, and I mean MUCH, better for being out of the castle, with good company and something fun to look forward to. The sun was shining, the sky was blue, there were one or two soft clouds floating by like inflatable sheep, and all in all everything was just dandy. One or two fluffy bunnies skittered among the flowers, and if I could smile, and had lips, a smile would have come to my lips.

'Oh, look,' cried Solstice. 'Fluffy bunnies. I do like fluffy bunnies. They're so uncool, they're cool.'

Little did we know then what significance
bunnies would soon have in our lives but, like
I said, it takes an Otherhand to really foul up
where a lesser mortal may just have made a
slight goof.

The only fly in the batter was, as usual,
from my point of view, the monkey. Fellah had
come along fairly happily, but halfway down the
road had started to get increasingly idiotic. He
pulled and tugged and squawked like I thought
only parrots could.

On we went, down into the valley and
along the road, and there, in the large pasture by
the head of the lake, was the circus.

It was a good spot for it, and there were
lots of people already arriving to see the show.

Having made a hasty retreat from the
castle, we'd arrived in plenty of time, and so we
decided to wander around the sideshows and
various stalls and other attractions of Wall's
Travelling Circus.

There was a lot to see, and of course,
everyone wanted to see something different.

'The Hall of Mirrors!' cried Solstice.

'The coconut shy!' announced

Grandma Slivinkov.

'The doughnut seller,' chipped in Cudweed, rather unsurprisingly.

'And I want to visit the fortune-teller,' finished Minty. 'So we'll all go and do what we want, but meet here again in half an hour! No later! The show starts at two and we want decent seats. Yes? Very well then, run along, run along.'

I sat on a tent pole and surveyed the scene.

Wall's was not a huge circus, by any means, but what it lacked in size it more than made up for in enthusiasm, variety, and downright oddness.

In the centre stood the big top, a super-big tent, with many poles, ropes, pegs and whatnot keeping it upright.

There were a dozen smaller tents, brightly coloured in broad red and gold stripes, and in each was some flim-flam or nonsense to amuse simple people and deprive them of their money. Cudweed was off, and wasted no time in parting with all his pocket money at the doughnut and candy floss stand. He dragged Fellah along, who was by now acting as though someone was drilling his tiny brain without mercy, pulling and tugging at his lead, and it was all Cudweed could do to shove some candy floss on the end of his nose, which distracted him briefly.

Solstice was more thoughtful, and strolled

about, wondering what to spend her money on. Should she try and win a nice pair of skull-print trainers on the hook-a-duck stall, or should she take a whirl on the ghoulish ghost train?

Grandma S was already hurling wooden balls at coconuts with alarming accuracy and violence, and Minty had vanished into a small green tent upon which hung a sign announcing:

Madame Zozo: Fortune- Teller to the Kings and Queens of Europe.

I saw some ugly-looking boys staring at me as I sat on my tent pole, and noticed they were holding a catapult. I know their sort only too well, and so hopped up into the air and set off to find Solstice, who was rather glum, as it turned out.

'Edgar,' she said, 'I really do not know what to spend my money on. Spooky trainers or a spooky train?'

'**Urk,**' I said, sympathising. It's a bad thing when indecision strikes, a bad thing indeed. I myself am often greatly vexed when faced with a rotting carcass and a dead mouse, as to which one to bury my beak in first. But there you go;

the trials of the raven are many.

'And it's nearly time for the show.
Now where has everyone got to?'

She was right.

Although Minty had set the time to meet,
she was late. Cudweed was nowhere to be seen
either. Eventually, Grandma and the horror
twins returned, and the show was about to start.
Finally Minty trotted up, looking rather puffed,
and puzzled, and very distracted. I think even
then we wondered what might be up with her,
but before anyone could ask, Cudweed arrived in
a great fluster.

'It's my monkey!' he declared wildly.
'He's got free! He legged it!'

'Now watch that slang, dear,' said Minty,

very absent-mindedly.

'But he's gone, Mother!' Cudweed bawled. 'Last time I saw him he was sitting in the candy floss machine. He'll get all sticky, and nobody likes a sticky monkey.'

'Well, it can't be helped,' she said firmly. 'The show is about to start and we don't have money to waste on tickets we don't use. We can find your wretched chimp later.'

'He's not a chimp, he's a monkey,' Cudweed protested. 'And I'm very worried about him.'

Solstice tried to soothe her brother's nerves.

'I'm sure we'll find him, brother Cudweed. He's most likely just had enough of the excitement and gone home. As long as he keeps out of Father's way he'll be fine. Really. You'll see.'

Cudweed didn't seem entirely convinced, but we managed to get him inside the tent.

There was a slight moment with the man taking the tickets at the entrance to the big top. I took one look at him and didn't like what I saw, and I think he did the same with me, because straight away he said, 'Where's his ticket?'

Odious ape. He was rather thin and long with nasty mean-looking eyes.

Minty laughed.

'Don't be silly. He doesn't need a ticket. He's only a bird.'

Only a bird! I'm a raven, and proud of it, I'll have you know. But I let it pass, because I did want to see the show.

'I don't care if he's the Queen of China, he still needs a ticket.'

'But that's preposterous. At these prices!'

'No ticket, no bird,' said the horrible man.

'Well, Mother,' said Solstice, 'maybe it would just be best to buy him a ticket . . . ?'

'Perhaps it would be best if Edgar waited outside and we can—'

I soon put a stop to that idea with a determined attack on Cudweed's head. It did the trick, and persuaded Minty that I needed a ticket of my own.

The grumpy ticket collector waved us through, pocketing more cash, and at last, there we all were, crowded onto the back row of seats.

The lights dimmed, a hush fell on the crowd.

The show began!

Three

Cudweed once
took up the violin,
but stopped when
someone asked who
was strangling
squirrels in the
music room.

It all began well enough.

The first act was a juggler, a permanently grinning buffoon, his smile plastered from one ear to the other, displaying many, many teeth. He juggled a succession of unlikely things, the finale involving chucking a squid, a cuttlefish and a small octopus above his head with rapid movements of the hands.

Cudweed was particularly impressed by this, and as the grinning performer left the arena, loudly declared that he wanted to be a juggler when he grew up.

Minty muttered something about Cudweed perhaps lacking sufficient deftness, but he didn't hear her, as into the big top strode a lion tamer, followed by a hungry-looking lion. After some basic moves, the lion tamer took his life in his hands and stuck his head between the lion's gaping jaws, to rapturous applause, at which point Cudweed announced that he wanted to be a lion tamer instead.

There followed a series of impressive acts; footballing dogs,

python charmers, counting horses, that kind of thing, and the fun was interrupted only by three clowns who were so embarrassingly bad that even children of five were booing them. When they cleared off, a troupe of five elephants began to skip and dance around the ring, as tumblers and acrobats leapt from back to back and tumbled around them.

A daring high wire act had Solstice gasping ('Gasp!' she said), and when it was over she could be heard wondering to anyone who'd listen whether you could get sparkly leotards in black instead of white.

Then there came a most excellent magician.

He wore a long black coat and sported a tall, black top hat. He made things appear, he made things disappear. He turned things into other things; he amazed and baffled and shocked and surprised, and he made us laugh. Well, that is to say, he made the rest of the audience laugh. Ravens don't do that sort of thing, but I did let out a cackle like a startled seagull as he whipped off his hat, and with a cry of 'Wugga-wugga-ding!' produced a sleepy, possibly drugged, white bunny from inside it.

Wugga Wugga DING

'Aaaaaaaaah!' went the crowd, in a how-sweet-kind-of-way.

However, the mood changed. Rapidly.

There was a commotion from behind the tent, and suddenly Fellah shot across the ring, screaming like an electrified poodle and running for his life. It seemed he was being chased by the spindly man; the grumpy ticket collector from earlier. He in turn was followed by a footballing dog. One of the goalkeepers, I think. People yelled a bit but they yelled a bit more as the dog was followed by a loose and lairy tiger. The tiger had a horse or three hard on his heels, and lastly four or five elephants trotted after them. A goat sauntered across the ring, oblivious to the whole dangerous business.

There was instant and total chaos as the mad chase hurtled around the ring, still led by Fellah who seemed to have the very devil inside his tiny nutcase.

'Aaaaaaaaah!' went the crowd, in a We're-all-going-to-die kind of way.

I thought it might be a good option to take to the skies, though my progress was limited by the mere fact that I was inside a tent. People yelled some more and ran for the exits, which was just as well, because about then, an elephant gaily tripped into one of the two main poles holding up the big top, and very soon, the big top was not up, but coming down around everyone's ears.

'Aaaaaaaaah!' yelled everyone, in an I-thought-there-was-some-chance-we-were-going-to-die-but-now-I'm-absolutely-sure kind of way.

Seeing a tiny gap, I fled for the safety of the outside world, and was pleased to find Solstice, Cudweed, Minty and the others all pulling themselves out from underneath a canvas flap.

'Gasp!' cried Solstice. 'That could have been nasty!'

'I think it is nasty,' Cudweed decided. 'Look!'

He was right. Underneath the deflated big top, hundreds of people were struggling and kicking and squawking and fighting to make their escape.

Minty nodded.

'I think Mr Box might have a busy afternoon, it's true.'

Cudweed squealed.

'Eeek! Fellah's still in there!'

I could only hope it was true.

Well, we had a long and agonising wait, during which Cudweed hopped about as though I was pecking his bottom, even though I wasn't.

Eventually however, the tent was taken down properly and all the survivors accounted for, and a few flattened things were hurriedly hurried away but nowhere, not anywhere, was there any sign of that confounded monkey. It seems he has a charmed life, a bit like a cat with nine lives, only much, much more irritating.

There was nothing else for it but to go home.

'Let's hope Father's in a better mood,' Solstice said to Grandma S as we went.

'Couldn't be worse, dear,' the mad old hag replied.

Minty nodded gloomily. She still seemed most out of sorts.

'And I was going to see Madame Zozo, the fortune-teller, again. She ran out of time just as she said she had something very interesting to tell me. Now I'll never know! And all because of your badly-behaved pet, Cudweed.'

She frowned, but it soon passed. She went on nattering to Grandma S, and Grandma S nattered back. It seemed that a few days hence, the twins, that terrible partnership of trouble, had reached the epic moment in their little lives of uttering their first words. Old lady Slivinkov, while impressed with this, had been less impressed by their choice of first words. While most children choose to utter 'mama!' or 'dada!' or perhaps 'more!' it seemed that Fizz had come out with 'fight!' and Buzz 'bite!' Or was it the other way round?

'Yes,' said Minty, agreeing with her mother, 'perhaps that isn't entirely normal . . .'

'Normal? Heh! Normal?' Grandma S. expostulated. 'No, it's not normal. I think I had better teach them something better to say, don't you, dear?'

Minty sighed. 'Very well, but be careful. We don't want to make things worse.'

I wondered what could be worse, but kept my beak shut. Instead, I sat on Cudweed's head to make him feel better about his missing monkey.

'I wonder what happened,' he said.

'At the circus?' Solstice asked. 'To go crazy?'

Cudweed nodded.

'You know,' he said, 'I was thinking. Remember when I got Fellah? From Catchem's pet shop?

That was just after the last time the circus came to town. You don't think . . . ?'

'I was wondering the same thing. Maybe he used to belong to the circus – maybe he escaped! Maybe that was why he didn't want to go today . . .'

'And maybe that was why that man was chasing him across the ring! Perhaps he spotted him and wanted him back! Coo. Just think. My monkey is an escaped and wanted criminal!'

'Well, not exactly a criminal,' Solstice said.

'Hmm. Perhaps not. But he is rather naughty.'

'Yes,' agreed Solstice. 'He is indeed rather naughty.'

That was true enough.

One visit to the circus and there were dozens dead and hundreds wounded. Rather, as we agreed, naughty.

But if that was naughty, it was nothing to the naughtiness that was soon to follow at Castle Otherhand, plunging the old place into a maelstrom of magic and mayhem.

Four

Several child
psychologists
have studied Fizz
and Buzz, each of
them declaring
that the twins
are unusually
unusual, even as
Otherhands go.

$\mathcal{B}$ut the mayhem didn't start

immediately. Nor did the magic. Before that,

there was at least one whole day of total boredom,

and as diverting as the trip to the circus had been,

I could feel the desperate urge to peck anything

and everyone rising inside my small black noodle

once more.

I took a spin of the castle to try and clear

my thoughts.

Sadly, the first thing I have to report is that

the monkey was safe and well. There he was,

sitting on the bust of Lord Deffreeque in

the Small Hall, which was doubly irritating,

because that's *my* favourite perching spot. One

of them, anyway, but that's not the point. The

point is that I had secretly been hoping
we'd been freed from the smelly
presence of the ape once and for
all, that he'd been trampled by an
elephant or swallowed by a python,
or torn to bits by a tiger, preferably
painfully.

Then we could have got
Cudweed a much nicer, and significantly
less smelly, pet. Something like a goldfish,
for example.

Ark!

Sadly, sadly not.

As soon as he saw him, Cudweed wailed
with delight, and the pair slunk off to his room,
no doubt to relish the excitement of the events at

the circus. Certainly Fellah was more animated than I think I've seen him before, which is really saying something, and gabbled away in his idiotic monkey language as they vanished upstairs.

Valevine, I presumed, was still ensconced in the East Tower with the mechanism for the accurate counting of cabbages. Minty went to have a long bath and the twins and Grandma went to an early bed.

Solstice had gone to her room, but the door was shut. I banged on it with the old beak and Solstice rushed to let me in, saying, 'Now for goodness' sake, Edgar, please don't start the pecking thing again.'

'**Ark!**' I declared, huffily. I'd had no intention of starting the *pecking thing* again.

Well not yet, anyway. All I wanted was some company at the end of a very trying day.

'Now, come on, Edgar,' Solstice cooed. 'Don't be a grumpy raven. Come and see what I'm looking at.'

I stalked over to the bed, where a huge book lay open. She lifted the cover to show me, her eyes wide.

'It's an old one of Mother's,' she whispered, then she whispered even more quietly, 'One of her spell books! She doesn't know I've got it! Don't tell, will you Edgar?'

'Cor,' I said, very slowly and quietly. None of my business, that was my basic view on the issue. Let the freaky family do what they like, as long as there's a ready supply of crisply dried

mice in my cage at the end of a long day's ravening.

'Good,' said Solstice. 'After all that fun with the magician at the circus, I thought I might try and learn a little magic, like Mother used to do when she was younger, you know.'

I did. Made me wince just to think of it.

'The only trouble,' she said, her face falling, 'is that it's all rather hard. Most of these spells have thousands of ingredients. Some only have a few but there are all these things I've never heard of. Pinkum root, for example. What's that? Bat noses! Where am I going to get little noses from little bats? And what on earth is Nooty powder?'

She sighed.

'And, furthermore, my mother's

handwriting is terrible. Terrible! I can barely read half the words in here. I've been looking at this thing for hours and, do you know, the only spell that I can read, I think, and for which I have all the ingredients, is this one, to stop rabbits eating the lettuces in your vegetable patch: *How to make Rabbits Hate Greens.* That's hardly very exciting is it?"

'**Awk!**' I agreed. It was not in the least bit exciting, but Solstice said she may as well learn it anyway, as it was somewhere to start.

I left her to it, and resumed my solitary prowl around the castle.

Night was coming on, and soon it would be time for all Otherhands to snuggle down and snooze their snoozy dreams.

All was quiet, all was calm.

And then I heard the sound of a duck. A duck, quacking. I could be quite sure about this because if there's one area of wildlife that ravens know about, it's our own nearest and dearest in the birding world.

So, yes, it was quite definitely a duck, and if you're thinking that's not so strange, I would have to agree with you, if the noise were coming from outside the castle walls.

But it was not, and though there are many types of duck to be found on Otherhand lake, this particular quacking came most definitely from inside the castle. Now, given that in my time I've contended with fang-beasts, guh-guh-ghosties, vampires and such-like terrors, I have to confess right here and now that I didn't pay the duck very much attention.

But that turned out to be a mistake.

A big one.

Five

Solstice's longest poem is four thousand lines long and took over her a year to write. The first word is Misery. The last is Gloom. The ones in between aren't much better.

Ravens are educated types, by and large.
We know rather a lot about some things, and
a little something about lots of other things.
It all works out rather nicely, but I have to
admit right now that I cannot think of the word
that describes a little mayhem. Not a lot of
mayhem, just a little. Not total chaos, just a
weeny bit of bother.

If you think of it perhaps you'd be good
enough to tell me, but in the meantime let me
continue with my account of what happened the
following morning, because although it could
not be said to be utter carnage yet, that was very
much the direction it was heading in . . .

Breakfast had not long been cleared
away, when there was a rather insistent knocking

at the front door.

I happened to be in the vicinity, and I perched like a wooden carving on the end of the staircase to see who would greet Flinch as that most concrete of butlers opened the door.

It was a lady, or a woman of sorts, and she was a stranger.

Or I thought she was, until Minty came by to see what was what.

'Why!' she cried. 'Madame Zozo!'

In the doorway stood the fortune-teller who Minty had seen at the circus yesterday. She dressed the way a fortune-teller should, with no definite sense of taste or colour, or the possibility that she might possess a mirror.

Random rags and strips of cloth were

draped around her head, many small dangly
things dangled from her fingers and ears and
well, almost anywhere where such things can
be fixed, and generally speaking she was quite
a piece of work.

'But, Madame Zozo!'
Minty declared. 'How did you
know where I live? I was going
to come and see you again after
the show yesterday, until that
silly misunderstanding with
the tent . . .'

Madame Zozo swept into
the room like an over-excited
vacuum cleaner.

'Yes!' she announced in

a most interesting and hitherto unheard accent, somewhere between Romanian and Welsh.

'Yes-yes! But Madame Zozo knows everything!'

Minty tittered. There is no other word for it; she tittered like a small and giggly schoolgirl.

'Everything?' came Valevine's voice. He was standing at the first-floor landing, taking a commanding view of the scene. Around him were several more cartloads of cabbages, on their way to the East Tower. 'Everything, you say? Ever-y-thing?'

He apparently did not have the same faith in Madame Zozo's talents that she herself had.

'Quite so,' announced Zozo coldly, glaring at Valevine. 'Quite. So.'

Valevine made a noise in his throat as

though he was swallowing frogs. His gaze swept

dismissively from Madame Z. to his butler.

'Flinch! Shut that blasted door, would you, and come and give me a hand here. In fact, better still, go and fetch a couple of boot boys and then all of you come and give me a hand, yes? Yes, good, that's the way.'

Madame Zozo was addressing Minty once more. Solstice and Cudweed drifted into the Small Hall to hear her declare that she had come to 'deliver a message from the heavens themselves' to Minty, to impart some great and wonderful knowledge that had been revealed to her, and which it was her duty to share with Lady Otherhand.

'Yes-yes! I saw it as you sat before me in my small and humble tent. And I knew you had to hear what the universe is telling you!'

That was too much for Valevine.

'What the universe is telling her? What the blasted universe is blasted telling her? I tell you this: never have I entertained such nonsense in this castle in my whole life! Never!'

'You silly man of small brain!' Zozo chided Valevine, pointing at Lord Otherhand in a most rude fashion. 'Do you think you know more than the universe does? Ha! No! The universe only shares its secrets with a chosen few.'

'A chosen few like you, I suppose?' Valevine countered, his eyebrows twitching madly.

'Now, dear,' said Minty, 'that's no way to talk to our guest.'

Valevine shot his wife a steely glare.

'Nonsense! The universe is telling you

nothing! If it did, I suppose you'd be able to make some wild prediction about the future.'

Well that seemed to be it for Madame Zozo, and closing her eyes she suddenly fell silent. She swayed slightly on her feet and then, making everyone jump out of their skins, her eyes sprang wide open again and she almost screamed.

'Dire calamity awaits! Terrible doom is coming. Right now!'

'Stuff and balderdash!' roared Valevine, and turned to pick up a box of cabbages at his feet. As he did so, however, in his haste, he tripped over another pile of the things, which started a chain reaction, sending a whole avalanche of cabbages hurtling down the stairs, just as the two boot boys were reporting for duty.

Death by cabbage. Well, it was not a very pleasant sight to behold, that's one thing, and another thing, which was nicely summed up by Solstice, was this:

'Gasp!' she whispered. 'Terrible doom awaits, eh? Gasp!'

But deadly cabbages were to be the least of our problems, and my poor little raven beak almost falls off with horror, as I think about it.

Six

A hundred years
ago, there was
a major storm,
during which
the Black Tower
collapsed. Its
ruins are now
one of Edgar's
favourite sulking
spots.

The rest of the day was strangely quiet.

Though it did smell of cabbage.

Valevine had left the scene of the accident and was tucked away once more in the laboratory.

Madame Zozo and Minty had vanished to some quiet and secret location where the fortune-teller could become 'better tuned to the infinite' or some such nonsense.

Futhork!

You might have guessed that I had already taken against Madame Zozo, and you might think this a little unfair, but I was with Valevine. He'd taken one look at the crazy coot and decided she was at best a nuisance and, at worst, trouble, and quite frankly so had I.

I had my reasons for this. I don't want

you to think that I take against any stranger who steps over the castle threshold, but come to think of it, given the number and variety of gold-diggers who come hunting for the Lost Treasure of Otherhand, that might not be such a bad idea.

And on top of any general suspicions I might have had, she had called me something bad as she left the Small Hall with Minty. She had called me a smelly crow. I ask you!

I just didn't like the look of her, and I think that's a pretty solid reason for disliking someone. I stared at her with a beady black eye.

Solstice got a bit cross with me.

'Honestly! Edgar! What *has* got into you? Where has all this rudeness suddenly come from?'

'Kawk!' I stated. 'Kaw-awk!'

'Don't speak to me like that,' Solstice chided. 'I don't know what's the matter with you, Edgar, but you can't just assume that any stranger who comes to the castle is up to no good.'

Can't I? I thought. Can't I? Given previous experiences, I think that would be a very good starting point. Hostility first! Then, if the newcomer turns out not to be an axe-loving maniac, or a murder merchant of some other sort, then, and only then, could we relax and give them a cup of tea and a nice iced bun.

Fair enough, no?

But Solstice was having none of it.

'Now I want you to be nice to Mother's friend, Edgar. And if you can't be nice, then for goodness' sake stop pecking and glaring at everyone and everything. Now, let's find that brother of mine and see what he's up to. He's been awfully quiet. He's up to something, I'm sure of it.'

Solstice was right. The boy had barely been seen ever since our return from the circus, and even then, only at mealtimes. Solstice knew her brother well, and it could mean only one thing: he was up to something.

We set off to investigate, and as we sauntered through the castle, the old place felt bigger and emptier than I had ever known it. Everyone was tucked away, busy scheming no doubt.

As we passed the nursery, we came across Grandma S and the twins.

Grandma S was not wasting her time with the twins. She had a row of tiny skulls laid out on the table, and was pointing at each in turn.

'One . . . two . . . three . . .' she was saying, slowly and stupidly, as if she was talking to a couple of toddlers, which I suppose in all fairness she was. 'One . . . two . . . three!'

She caught sight of Solstice and me in the doorway and broke off.

'Heh!' she announced. 'Just teaching the little ankle-biters to count.'

'Grandma!' exclaimed Solstice. 'What an unusually helpful thing to do! What a good idea! How's it . . . you know, how's it going?'

'Heh,' declared the aged grandparent. 'We're having a few problems. Watch.'

She carefully pointed at each skull in turn, once again, and began to count, very solemnly.

'One . . . two . . . three . . .'

Then Fizz and Buzz very carefully pointed at each skull in turn, and with a look of enormous concentration spread across each of their little faces, counted back.

'One . . . one . . . one . . .'

They beamed.

Grandma S turned to us with an air of desperation.

'We've been at this rather some time now,' she said, her voice a little frailer than usual. 'Come on, dears, try again. One . . . two . . . three . . .'

And try again they did.

'One . . . one . . . one . . .'

Buzz picked up one of the skulls and began to suck it.

Fizz pointed at Grandma, Solstice and then me.

'One . . . one . . . one . . .' she said. She beamed again.

Grandma S let out a tiny sob and Solstice

and I made our excuses and left before we got involved.

We came to Cudweed's room, and Solstice was just about to knock on the door when, quite clearly, a duck quacked on the other side.

'Cudweed?' called Solstice. 'Is that you?'

Not her finest moment, but I knew what she was getting at; viz, do you have a duck in your room?

'Cudweed! May we come in? It's Edgar and me.'

There was a slight scuffling and a couple of very audible quacks.

'Wait a minute!' Cudweed's voice came through the woodwork. He sounded bothered. 'Wait a minute!'

There was more scrabbling and then one final, and very loud, quack.

The door opened and Cudweed shoved his rather hot-looking face through the crack.

'Yes?' he said, trying and failing to adopt an air of calm. 'Can I help you?'

Solstice was having none of it, but neither was Cudweed. The door stayed where it was.

'What do you mean, "Can I help you?". You don't own a shop! I'm your sister and I want to talk to you. Is that so odd?'

'No,' said Cudweed. 'But it's not convenient at the moment.'

Solstice was about to open her mouth but was beaten to it by a beak, and not mine, for once.

Quack!

'What,' asked Solstice, 'was that? Exactly?'

'What?' asked Cudweed, looking guiltier than even a very guilty boy has any right to.

'That quack,' Solstice stated. 'Have you got a duck in there?'

'No!' cried Cudweed.

Quack!

'Eek!' squealed Cudweed, 'Fellah's at it again!'

With that he disappeared inside his room, slamming the door behind him.

Seven

Solstice hasn't
yet decided
what to do with
her life when
she grows up.
She only knows
it had better
involve wearing
black.

The thing about ravens is that they don't take no for an answer.

Persistence is our watchword, perseverance is our middle name.

We just simply do not quit.

So when Cudweed shut the door in our faces, I took one look at Solstice, and she nodded.

'All right, Edgar. You can forget everything I said about not pecking things any more. Let him have it.'

I didn't need telling twice, and I set about that door as if a pneumatic drill had been glued to my face. It was enough to drive anybody crazy, but especially a nervy ten-year-old boy with something to hide.

Furthermore, it appeared that my pecking had started some other kind of commotion inside his bedroom, involving the squawking of monkeys, the quacking of a duck, and an awful lot of capering about.

The din was terrible and, fearing that the whole castle would hear, Cudweed was forced to open the door within a mere couple of minutes.

'Stop!' he wailed. 'Solstice! Make him stop!'

'Very well,' Solstice agreed, patting me on the head, my signal to cease fire. 'Very well, but let us in now and no more nonsense with shut doors, all right?'

Cudweed nodded meekly and let us into his room, glancing up and down the corridor as he did so, checking for wayward parents, or even, and I shudder to think about it, the towering form of Nanny Lumber, though fortunately for the whole castle, she'd been in bed for a couple of weeks with a severe attack of woodworm. The doctor had prescribed daily dippings in preservative but her response to this treatment was, I'm glad to report, slow.

Nevertheless, Cudweed was looking pretty worried, and we soon saw why.

Fellah was chasing a small but angry duck around the room.

'Fellah! Stop that!'

Cudweed lunged towards his monkey,

knocking a couple of lamps flying. He managed
to grab the primate's tail and wrestle him to
the ground.

'Bad monkey!' Cudweed said, sternly.

The duck settled down, and stood in
a corner of the room, watching everyone with
one shining eye, and preening himself with a
spectacular air of indignation.

'And who, or what, I should say,' said
Solstice, 'is that?'

She pointed at the duck.

'What? Who? Oh, him?'

'Yes, *him*.'

'He's my new pet,' Cudweed said innocently, 'He's called Mucky Duck.'

'Mucky Duck?' exclaimed Solstice. 'And who exactly is Mucky Duck?'

'Oh,' explained Cudweed carefully, 'he's just a duck.'

'I see,' said Solstice. 'And do I take it that Mother and Father are, how shall I put this, unaware of the existence of Mucky Duck?'

Cudweed nodded, sheepishly, it must be said.

'Er,' he said. 'Yes.'

'Is that a tremendously good idea?' Solstice said. She went to have a good look at Mucky Duck, who gave a very quiet little quack in return.

'Your own name, is it?' she asked.

Cudweed brightened up quite a lot.

'Oh yes!' he said. 'Good isn't it? You'll never guess how I thought of it!'

'Is it because he makes a mess everywhere?'

'Oh,' said Cudweed, looking rather crestfallen again. 'Yes. How did you guess?'

Solstice looked at Cudweed's room.

I would just like to add a small footnote here that my own behaviour is not carried out in such a fashion, if you get what I mean. You don't? Please don't be coy, I'm sure you realise I'm talking about an entirely natural process and I'm simply trying to point out that I take care of my own natural processes outside, and well away from the castle. The duck, however, did not seem to have the same good manners.

'Just a wild stab in the dark,' Solstice said, wrinkling her nose. 'Anyway, mess apart, it's a very nice name, so well done you. The only trouble

is, how on earth do you think you're
going to get away with it? Fellah's bad
enough but with the two of them and all
this monkey-duck nonsense going on, you're
heading for trouble, Cudweed. Big trouble.'

Cudweed looked worried, chewing his
bottom lip.

'Where did he come from, anyway?'
Solstice continued. 'I thought you were having
enough fun with Fellah. And now this duck!
Where did you get him?'

'Oh,' said Cudweed, 'I just sort of got
him. You know.'

I did not know and I don't think Solstice
did either, but there were other things to worry
about just then.

'It's simply not going to work,' she said. 'You'll get found out and then one of them will have to go. And which of the two of them will you choose?!'

'The three of them,' Cudweed said quietly.

Solstice spun round.

'What did you say? The *three* of them?'

'Yes,' repeated Cudweed. 'The three of them.'

And at that point, I let out a squawk, because I had just spotted another small creature. It was sitting on Cudweed's head, and at first glance it appeared to be a rather large hamster wearing a very small top hat, and a miniature black dinner jacket.

Solstice had seen it too.

'And what, or rather who,' she groaned, 'is that?'

'This is my new hamster,' Cudweed said. 'He's called Mr Whiskers. I called him that because . . .'

'Yes, I can guess,' interrupted Solstice. 'Oh, Cudweed! What are we going to do? You simply will not be allowed to keep this . . . this . . . zoo!'

I had to agree with Solstice.

Cudweed seemed to have made a grave miscalculation, thinking he might get away with a menagerie in his bedroom. But if he'd made a miscalculation, then we'd made an even bigger one, the upshot of which was very soon to shoot up, spreading chaos throughout the land of Otherhand.

Eight

One very cold
winter the whole
of Otherhand
lake froze,
and Valevine
produced one
of his most
successful, but
most lethal,
inventions:
rocket-powered
ice-skates.

I flew.

Just for the sheer hell of it, and I realised what a long time it had been since I'd actually just flown nowhere in particular, with nothing to do and no goal in mind.

It was a lovely hot summer's day and I soared into the heavens, drifting higher and higher on thermals of hot air that rose from the valley floor.

I was startled by a glider – one of those rather pointless planes without engines that people insist on cluttering the sky with on summer's days like this one. Being silent, it crept up behind me unawares, and as it swooshed past it fairly took the wind out of my sails.

That rather got my goat, and I flew after

it and swooped on it from behind in return, and
then set about pecking the plastic roof of the
cockpit with demonic fury.

The pilot seemed a little surprised, but
there was nothing he could do. After a while,
however, I heard Solstice's voice float into my
head, and I found I had to agree with her.

Where was all this pecking coming from? The last time I remember being quite so bonkers was when I was a tiny and frequently grumpy ravenlet, and I suddenly wondered if I was reverting to childhood in my old age, losing a few straws from my hay-stack. In short, going senile. It was not a comforting thought.

So I stopped pecking and then, while I was thinking about all this, I was aware that I had stopped flapping too, and was tumbling towards the ground faster than a pig in a bag. A heavy pig.

Feeling that this rather proved the case about me being senile, I grudgingly started flapping again and headed back to the castle before I did myself any serious damage.

I told myself I wasn't getting old in the head, I was merely preoccupied. The castle has seen such a series of odd and strange events of late, and somehow I knew we were heading for another one.

I did not trust Madame Zozo.

That was it. Admitting that to myself made me feel better, but it was no more than a feeling; there was nothing to suggest that she was anything other than what she claimed to be, and after all, even if there was, what could I do about it?

My suspicions were confirmed at dinner time.

I think we'd all expected Madame Z. to have said her piece, received a palmful of silver coins in true gypsy fortune-teller fashion, and been well on her way by tea-time. But no!

Here she was, sitting at Minty's right hand at the dinner table.

And everyone was passing the salt and chinwagging just as merrily as you please. Everyone except Valevine, who didn't share his wife's welcoming nature. But, that said, he wasn't kicking up a fuss either about this new guest, and seemed to be in his own little world, no doubt one full of cabbages.

I thought about pecking Madame Zozo to see if I could get her to confess she was actually a gold-hunter, but Solstice knows me too well and from the look in my eye she knew what I had planned.

'Edgar,' she warned, wagging a finger at me, 'no. Play nicely like a good raven.'

'**Ark**,' I said. '**Ark**.' Which meant, basically, well all right then, but if she gives me the slightest reason to be suspicious I'm going into battle mode with the old beak and no one's going to stop me. See?

I think that was clear, but what also became clear was that Madame Zozo would be staying the night.

It transpired that the 'mystical universe' was 'out of alignment' on this particular day, and as a result, Madame Zozo was unable to impart whatever earth-shattering news she had for Minty at the present time. Minty therefore had invited Zozo to stay for the night.

'Or as long,' she chimed, beaming at her new friend, 'as it jolly well takes until the universe is playing ball again. Yes? Isn't that wonderful, dear?'

Looking for support, she turned to Valevine, who merely muttered, 'cabbages', more to himself than to anyone else I think.

Minty turned to Solstice and Cudweed.

'Children? Isn't it exciting having a fortune-teller in the house? Yes?'

Solstice nodded, and Cudweed, who was on his best behaviour, piped up, 'Yes, Mother. I think it's *really* good. It's a *really* good idea of yours. *Really* good.'

He was clearly on a campaign of top-notch manners, presumably to try and gain some credit for the inevitable moment when Mucky Duck was found. And Mr Whiskers.

Madame Zozo was all smiles.

She gazed round at the family, grinning

from ear to ear.

'How charming!' she declared. 'How charming! And I shall be delighted to stay for as long as the naughty old universe decides is right! Shan't that be lovely?'

No, I thought, it shall not.

I didn't know what it was about her, but I just did not trust her.

Not one teeny bit.

Nine

One of the worst treasure hunters ever to make a bid for the Otherhand treasure was Clumsy Clive. He broke his ankle on one of Spatchcock's turnips before he'd even set foot inside the castle.

Well, Madame Zozo might have fooled her way into Minty's good books, and sneaked herself into an overnight stay at Castle Otherhand, but if she was up to something, she'd have me to contend with.

Nothing, and nobody, I told myself, is going to make a monkey out of this raven, if you'll pardon the mixation of species. And once I make up my mind about something, that's it. No doubts, no second thoughts for me. Just rapid thinking and rapider action.

I would stand vigil, all night if necessary, at Zozo's door. If she came out, I'd see her. If she so much as sneezed I'd know about it. If she even thought of doing something wicked, I'd be there to hear her thoughts.

However, I am a sensible bird, and I thought it would be a good idea to make sure I was properly prepared for the long, bold and noble task ahead. Before I set up shop outside the guest room to which Zozo had been assigned, I headed for the kitchens, in search of tasty titbits.

Now this is something I often get up to. Sneaking into the larders, I mean. Because although I am unusually fond of the dried mice Solstice brings me, even the dullest of birds would get fed up with just one source of protein, correct?

Therefore, I like to make frequent excursions into the kitchens in search of a wider variety of goodies. It does mean ducking and diving a little, and this evening was no exception

as Cook waved a toasting fork
at me and threatened to bake
me in a pie.

She was no match for my superior
aerobatics, however, and I wove and frolicked
around the fork, leaving her quite in a spin and,
seeing my way clear to the larder door, I executed
my finest manoeuvre, in which I dive-bomb just
hard enough on the handle of the door, execute
a small hopping action, and hey
presto! The larder, and
all its secret treasures,
are mine!

Sadly,
however, though I
carried out this nifty

piece of footwork with no problem, I had not counted on what lay behind the door.

Cook rushed up, screaming as the door swung open.

'Nooooo! Edgar! Nooooo!'

It was a close thing, and I shudder to think about it now, as about four thousand cabbages tumbled out of the larder, like a vegetable tidal wave, a green and smelly onslaught, that swept everything before it, nearly including your favourite raven.

Fortunately I still have a trick or two under my wing, and was able to pull off a rather neat little barrel roll, which not only got me out of trouble, but with some style too, I'm pleased to say. Well, you never know who might be watching.

Now, I might have been finished with the cabbages, but the cabbages were far from finished themselves.

They had presumably been sent to the larder after squashing the two boot boys, and now, bounding out of it like over-excited Labrador puppies, they found themselves thundering joyously towards the top of the back entrance to the cellars.

Well, they didn't need telling twice. Off they went, and I suppose all would have been well if it were not for the fact that a poor kitchen maid was just returning back up the cellar steps at that very moment, having been sent to fetch more candles.

Now, I wouldn't want you to think I'm cold-hearted or anything, but I do have to confess that in the ensuing pandemonium, following the third cabbage-related death in twenty-four hours, I took the opportunity to have a good forage in the back of the larder. I came away with a few things much more interesting than greens; for example, some dried ham, a nice piece of mouldy parmesan cheese, and some black olives.

I spent about half an hour ferrying these items from the larder to the perch I'd selected opposite Madame Zozo's door, and all was ready.

As I passed through the Small Hall on my final trip, I overheard Minty on the phone to Box and Sons.

'Yes, I know it's late,' she was saying, 'Yes, I know. No, I wouldn't have thought cabbages were that lethal either. No, the large sort. But there you go. Very well. Nine o'clock sharp. Thank you very much.'

Valevine stood nearby muttering loudly to nobody in particular.

'Hah!' he said. 'I think all this rather proves my point. The sooner we get these blasted vegetables counted, the sooner we can sleep safely in our beds! Yes? Hah!'

He swaggered round the room looking for someone to accost but fortunately no one was there to be accosted.

They are all as mentally disturbed as each other, these Otherhands. Disturbed, and dangerous. That's one thing I've learned over the years.

Give them a soft bag of extra-soft cotton wool and they could still probably contrive some way of badly injuring a butler with it.

But enough! I'm rambling, and there's no time for that sort of thing.

So, I thought, as I took up my perch above Zozo's door, just you try and get out of there without me seeing. Just you try.

I sat for a bit, nibbling on this, chewing on that, and, after a very long time waiting, absolutely nothing happened.

I sat for a bit more, pecking on the parmesan, but more to show willing than from any actual hunger, and a thought occurred to me.

It was possible, I thought, *just* possible, that I had got to the perchy-point a weeny bit late.

By the time I'd made my last run from the larder, it was *just* conceivable that Zozo had already snuck out to get up to whatever no-goodness it was she was getting up to.

Hum, I thought. That would leave a small hole in my otherwise watertight plan.

But then, a-ha!

Another thought followed hard on the heels of the first, namely, that even if she had already slunk into the castle, she would have to come back, and o-ho! Then I'd have her, for sure.

I know my genius is a little bit off-putting sometimes, so I won't bang on about it, but honestly, I was really rather proud of my old black brain box.

So my plan was watertight and ship-shape

once more, or rather it would have been, but for one thing.

I think, that is to say, I know, that I fell asleep.

Futhork! What a stupid old bird I am sometimes.

And I think I'd eaten a bit too much cheese, because, boy! Did I have some weird dreams that night. I don't know if you're aware of this odd gastronomic phenomenon, but if not, you really ought to try it some time. Eat too much cheese before bed, shut the old eyelids, and await spectacular results.

Never fails!

It also works with rotting porcupine, three-day-dead hedgehog, and weevil juice.

That's the goo you often find seeping out of a weevil nest, in case you're thinking of trying it . . .

But parmesan is simply dandy too, and works a treat.

Just before I woke, for example, I had a really strange dream, in which I was perched above someone's door in the castle, when all of a sudden a white bunny hopped past me, quite gaily, down the length of the carpet.

Not so odd, you say? Well it wouldn't have been, except that the first bunny was followed by a second, and the second by a third, and . . .

You get the idea. I must have seen a thousand of the things hop by me as I dozed.

Most odd dream.

Most odd.

And as I woke, I wondered what it
meant. As it turned out, I didn't have to wait too
long to find out.

Ten

Christmas is always
good fun at the
castle. A huge tree
is brought in from
the forest, so tall
that to decorate it
requires stable boys
to climb up through
its branches, placing
a shiny skull at the
very top.

Small boys.

It occurs to me that I should say something on the subject of small boys and, especially, on the subject of how a small boy is able to create fuss and bother, anywhere, any time, in even the least likely situations.

Put a small boy in an empty room, shut the door and leave him alone for ten minutes and when you get back you'd better be prepared for a lot of mess, a great deal of noise, and some smells you've never come across before too.

Now, if you add into the mix a wide variety of small but jittery creatures, then you can imagine the equally wide variety of disasters that can, and usually do, follow.

All this was something on which we were

about to have a lesson or two, but we had a taster session at breakfast, the morning after my lonely vigil outside Madame Zozo's room. It began peacefully enough, but this was merely the calm before the storm.

Minty was trying to make bright conversation, in order to make Madame Zozo feel more at home, I think, though to be honest, she was very much making herself at home anyway, if you ask me. She was wading her way through a third helping of bacon and eggs, and I was watching the rashers in the serving dish disappear all too rapidly.

I squawked a bit every time she took more, trying to get people to notice, but no one did.

Madame Zozo had already announced

that it seemed unlikely that she would be able to divulge Minty's great and wonderful 'message from the stars' that day, or even possibly the next. Now I took all this as very suspicious, but no one else seemed bothered in the least.

'How are your cabbages this morning, husband dear?' Minty asked Valevine, but our lord and master seemed very out of sorts. I was actually getting a bit worried about the old lunatic, which is really saying something, given the kind of idiocy we're used to from the direction of the East Tower.

Valevine raised his head from his porridge and growled.

'Green.'

Minty forced a smile.

'That's very interesting,' she ventured to Solstice and Cudweed, 'Don't you think, dears?'

Solstice did not bother to reply, and Cudweed, well, Cudweed seemed to go pale, and his eyes appeared to be about to pop out of his head, which is not a normal reaction to being asked about vegetables, even the scariest of vegetables.

Do you know what the scariest vegetable is, while the subject has come up?

Well, I don't want to take up too much of your time, but since you ask, it's the Brussel sprout. Why?

Because they taste horrible?

Because they smell?

Because if you're not careful an undercooked one can take your eye out, as it pings off your fork?

Well, perhaps all these things are true and add a certain extra element of fear to the nasty little mini-freak cabbages, but no! The actual reason is much more sinister . . .

Let me compare the human species to the Brussel sprout. Every human being, in all their variety, everyone alive today, everyone who's ever lived, their entire being has been determined by the presence of just forty-six chromosomes inside the nuclei of their cells . . . Just forty-six!

The Brussel sprout, on the other hand, has one hundred and thirty-two. Which rather begs the question; *what are they doing with them all?* Deciding to be slightly greener? Or slightly more smelly?

Possibly, but it's my firm and long-held belief that the sprout is in fact secretly a race of super-intelligent and evil beings, just waiting for the right moment to rise from the Christmas dinner table and take over the world.

You see if I'm not wrong!

All this is *absolutely* true by the way, but it has rather got me off the subject of breakfast, and Cudweed going pale.

Now, at about the same moment that his eyes started popping, Valevine raised his gaze from his bowl and said one more single word.

'Rabbit.'

'What, dear?' Minty said.

'I said, rabbit,' he said, and pointed.

'Flinch! Sort it out, will you?'

Everyone followed Valevine's carefully directed digit, and there, at the far end of the dining hall, sat a large white bunny, as proud as you like.

'Yessir,' rumbled Flinch, and began to solemnly stagger down the considerable length of the room towards the rabbit.

He was a couple of arms' lengths away, however, when the naughty bunny ducked through the doorway and out of sight.

'Dear me,' grumbled Flinch, but the pesky pet hadn't gone for good.

'There he is!' cried Solstice, as quick as ever, but not as quick as the bunny, who had somehow reappeared at the far end of the dining room, a short jog away.

'Flinch!' roared Valevine, and once more the splendorously clumsy butler began to lope towards the rabbit.

No sooner had he got within snatching distance, however, than the cheeky creature disappeared once more.

'Now he's there again!' cried Solstice, spotting the rabbit back in his starting place. 'Gasp! He got there quickly. What a super speedy bunnikins!'

'I'll help!' shouted Cudweed and, ignoring protests from his mother, began to scamper as fast as he could towards the bunny, knocking into Flinch as he went. The pair stumbled on, and for a third time that bold and bouncy rabbit vanished from sight.

'Now where's he gone?' roared Valevine.

'The fireplace!' announced Madame Zozo, and before Flinch and Cudweed could react, a couple of maids and an under-butler named Bunsen were all hurtling after it.

I shan't detain you with more details, but before very long there was a rambunctious chase in full swing round the breakfast table, culminating, and this is very much the point, in a small accident that went unseen by everyone.

Everyone, that is, except me.

For as the hunt rounded the table for the fifth or sixth time, someone knocked into the back of Madame Zozo and, as they did so, I saw what no one else saw; that Madame Zozo's hair slipped down her face!

She quickly
snatched it up again,
and straightened it on
her head once more,
but it was clear to
me that the peculiar
teller of fortunes was
wearing a wig!

Now why might
that be, I wondered?

Could there be an innocent explanation,
such as she lost all her hair, in a game of poker,
for example?

Or could there be a more sinister answer
to this conundrum?

Could it be, perhaps, that Madame Zozo was actually trying to conceal her true identity?

Time was very soon to tell.

Yes indeed!

The bunny, in case you're wondering, made a clean escape, and was not seen again. Well, not for a few hours at least.

Eleven

Cudweed's favourite room in the castle is the armoury – he loves looking at all the old weapons, trying to imagine how much they hurt.

A rather nifty plan formed in my noggin. That is to say, somewhere within the tiny space inside my feathery head, a notion appeared, and I thought it to be a good one.

My plan was this. I would follow Madame Zozo, for the whole day, minute after minute, hour after hour, and I would wait for another slip, some other clue that she was up to no good, and then perhaps I'd have her!

It was a good plan; its strength was its simplicity, and it worked for precisely twenty minutes until Minty and Zozo retired to the Black Room, and shut the door in my face.

'Sorry Edgar,' Minty said, 'But Madame is quite insistent that we should have total silence and utter privacy in which to await the arrival of my heavenly fortune. You understand?'

I did not, but what could I do short of start another pecking session? Which had got me precisely nowhere last time anyway.

As they shut the door on me, I heard Minty telling Madame Zozo what a good friend she was.

'It's almost as though we've met before, I feel I know you so well.'

'Oh, how charming, charming,' gushed the flouncy fortune-teller.

So my entrance was blocked.

But barred as I was from the Black

Room, they seemed to have forgotten that the room has several windows, and I should soon be found perching outside, my earhole pressed to the glass.

I set off down the corridor, steering my way here and there, trying to find an exit to the outside world, but it appeared to be one of those days when the castle was not playing ball, because despite the fact that it was warm outside, I could not find a single open window.

Sometimes this happens to me, and you must understand that my life on a day-to-day basis can be dictated by the fact that the only door in the castle that I can open is the one to the larder, and even that took me years to figure out, though as you can imagine I did have a very good incentive.

I'd almost given up when I found myself gliding down the Long Gallery, a splendid and fine hall with paintings of many and various Otherhand ancestors upon the walls. I saw Solstice and was a little surprised, for this was not one of her usual haunts.

'Oh! Edgar!' she called, seeing me approach.

I slid to a halt mid-air and dropped onto her outstretched wrist.

'Edgar, dear, you haven't seen Father anywhere around, have you?'

'Awk!' I declared.

'No, I thought not, but he's here somewhere. He keeps calling me and I've been trying to find him but I can't. I . . .'

'Solstice!'

It was the voice of Lord Otherhand, and though he was nowhere to be seen, his voice seemed to be coming from the far end of the Gallery.

We set off in the direction of the voice.

'See what I mean, Edgar?'

'Ark!' I agreed.

'Yes, and every time I follow his voice, he's not there any more.'

The voice came again, from just round the corner of the hallway.

'Solstice. Come here, daughter of mine!'

But as soon as we got there, Valevine had gone.

'I think he's playing games,' Solstice said. '**Kar-kark!**' I muttered. I have to say that playing games seemed unlikely for Lord Otherhand, especially when there were cabbages to be counted and machines to be made to do the job.

'Solstice! Come here, daughter!'

Once more we heard Valevine's voice calling and we began to follow. We turned several more corners, but just as we thought we must be about to find Lord Otherhand waiting for us, tapping his feet and bristling his eyebrows, we didn't.

He simply wasn't there.

And then things got even weirder.

We were approaching the corridor which led first to Cudweed's and then Solstice's rooms, and from one particular window there's a pretty good view across the courtyard and up to the East Tower.

And there, high in the Tower, and even though it was a good long way away, I swear that I could see Lord Valevine in his laboratory, doing laboratorial things, as usual.

And yet we'd heard his voice only moments before we turned the last corner.

It was too much for my poor little brain to cope with.

Rurk! Rark rurk!

I thought it was worth making it clear to Solstice what I had seen and so I pecked on the window, but as soon as I did that she thought I was going loopy again and got a bit cross.

'Please, Edgar,' she moaned. 'We can't start all that again.'

'Ark!' I squawked. I'd only been trying to point out the weird thing about her father, but she wasn't listening.

Then! Blow me down!

We heard Valevine's voice again, and it seemed to come from a little way down the corridor, from inside Cudweed's bedroom.

Well, this time, Solstice didn't even

bother knocking. Determined to get to the bottom of the mystery, she barged straight through the door, and we got quite a surprise.

We did not find Valevine, as we expected.

What we found was Cudweed, looking more than a little worried, shameful, and guilty too.

At first I thought it had snowed in Cudweed's room and then, realising it was June and, furthermore, that we were inside, I discounted that possibility.

What I took to be snow was, in fact, rabbits.

White ones.

His entire room was filled, from corner to corner, with large white rabbits, and rabbits were precisely the only thing you could see in his room.

Just rabbits.

Except for a snazzily-dressed hamster,
and a bird.

'Quack,' said Mucky Duck, poking
his head out from behind two particularly
large bunnies.

He didn't sound happy.

Twelve

Apart from
her bedroom,
Solstice's
favourite room in
the castle is the
Glass Gallery,
an amazing
conservatory of
strange plants
and fantastic
trees, many with
tendrils like
tentacles.

There was a long silence, during which Cudweed looked at Solstice, and Solstice looked at Cudweed. I looked at the pair of them, wondering who was going to speak first, but it seemed they were both lost for words.

I noticed that Cudweed's mouth was open and his lower jaw was moving up and down slightly, as if he was trying to get some words out, but none came.

In the end, I supplied what I feel was the only appropriate thing to say.

Futhork!

Solstice looked at me sternly.

'I suspect that's not a very nice word,' she said. 'I suspect it's not the sort of word that nice ravens were brought up to say. But actually, as it happens, I agree with you. Futhork, Cudweed! What on earth are you doing? And where, oh where, did all the rabbits come from?'

Cudweed looked worried, as I've mentioned, but somehow at the same time he seemed extremely pleased with himself.

'You couldn't shut the door, could you? Nic Nac's trying to escape,' he said, pointing at a sneaky bunny who was about to make a dash for freedom.

'You have no idea,' he went on, 'how hard it is keeping them all in here. Nic Nac's always trying it, but he's not the worst.'

'The worst?' asked Solstice, still open-mouthed in wonder and horror at the sheer quantity of rabbits jostling for floor space in Cudweed's room.

'Oh yes,' Cudweed explained, with quite the air of the professor about him. 'You see, some are much worse than others. Some keep trying to escape, like Nic Nac, Odin and Sassafrass. Whereas some of the others seem quite happy to sit it out in my room, like Merripit, Tornado and Telstar, over there. You wouldn't believe—'

Here, Solstice interrupted him.

'Wait, wait, wait!' she cried. 'There's something I need to get absolutely clear here. Are you saying, as I think you might be implying to us, that you have a name for each and every one of these bunnies?'

'Oh, yes,' said Cudweed, as if his sister was slightly slow.

'Every single one?'

'Oh, yes,' Cudweed repeated.

'And you can tell them apart, can you?'

'Oh,' said Cudweed, 'yes.'

'So,' said Solstice, whirling about and pointing at a bunny which looked precisely the same as all the rest. 'Who's that?'

'Oh! That's Voodoo,' said Cudweed.

'Voodoo? Very well. And who's that?'

'Mycroft.'

'And that?'

'Mic Mac.'

'I thought the one by the door was Mic Mac?'

'No, silly, that's Nic Nac.'

'Of course, silly me,' said Solstice, sounding ever more desperate. 'And that one?'

'Jester.'

'And him.'

'Bellamy.'

'That one?'

'That's Telstar, you goose, I already introduced him,' said Cudweed, adding suspiciously, 'Are you trying to catch me out?'

Solstice threw her hands in the air.

'Oh, Brother! Far from it. I am simply amazed by your ability to not only name all these rascals, but to tell them all apart. How do you do it?'

Cudweed shrugged.

'I don't know. I just look at their little faces and a name pops into my head.'

'But there must be . . . a hundred of them in here!'

'Three hundred and forty-three,' Cudweed said quietly. 'Actually.'

Solstice was silent. Cudweed shrieked.

'Starlight! Leave Titan alone! Stop that right now. That's very naughty. Naughty bunny!'

'Cudweed,' Solstice said, trying to get his attention, but the deluded child was in his element now.

'Yes, you see, that's Nub, and there's Rumpus, Grimpen, Kennedy and Odiemon. Then we have Aulrick, Frazzle and—'

'Cudweed!' Solstice said firmly.

'And there's Danny, and Tricky Rich, and Jeffrey, and Silvertoes, and Hullaballoo, and Quarrel, and—'

'Cudweed!' Now Solstice screamed so loud I thought the castle would fall down about our ears. It didn't, but she did get Cudweed to stop telling us the names of his blasted bunnies.

'Yes?' he asked, looking a little offended.

'Enough! That's simply enough! I do not wish to know the names of all your rabbits and even if I did there's no way I would be able

to remember them all. But that is not the point.
At all. I have two questions for you, and I would
be very grateful if you would be so kind as to
give these questions your full, and I do mean
full, attention. Is that acceptable to you, my
little brother?'

Cudweed blinked.

'Yes,' he said, looking rather grumpy
now. I felt sorry for the small chap, though that
lessened slightly when I felt something else: a
bunny nibbling my tail feathers. I took a perch
on top of Cudweed's
bookcase, safely
out of the reach of
rabbit. Or indeed, hamster.
Or duck.

'My first question is, and I would very much appreciate an honest answer, where did all the bunnies come from? Where?'

Cudweed grinned, then realised that might not be helping his cause, and tried to wipe the smile from his face.

'Well,' he said, 'You remember that we went to the circus?'

'I am not entirely dim, brother dear; it was only a couple of days ago.'

'Yes,' Cudweed continued, 'And you remember how Fellah got upset and disappeared?'

'Yes, I remember that too,' Solstice said.

'But now you mention it, where is Fellah anyway?'

'He's not too keen on all my new pets,' Cudweed said sadly. 'I expect he's not far away really. Anyway, you remember how at the circus there was all that funny, I mean *terrible*, business when Fellah ran across the ring? Well, somewhere in all the bother he picked something up, and when I got back to the castle I found him. With this thing. You see?'

'Possibly,' said Solstice. 'What, precisely, is this thing?'

'Ah, well, I was coming to that.'

Slowly, I thought, but I let the boy finish.

'You see, the thing Fellah stole, I mean, brought back from the circus, was the magician's hat. His hat. You see?'

'Oh, Cudweed,' said Solstice very carefully. 'What have you done?'

Cudweed had the decency to look slightly guilty.

'I made a few rabbits.'

'A few?!'

'And a hamster.'

'Mr Whiskers?'

'And a duck.'

'Quack,' said Mucky Duck.

Thirteen

As a young girl,
Minty loved
riding horses,
and won several
prizes on her
horse, Thunder,
until she was
accused of
casting spells on
the other horses,
in order to win.

'**I** haven't asked my second question yet,' Solstice said, 'but before I do, I have another question.'

'That makes three questions, doesn't it?' asked Cudweed, sounding worried.

'It does,' admitted Solstice, 'but it's only because your answer to my first question has brought up something else that needs to be answered.'

Cudweed regarded his sister with suspicion.

'That could go on for ever though,' he said, wrestling his way through a sea of large white bunny rabbits. 'Couldn't it?'

Solstice wisely chose to ignore him and instead dived straight in with her bonus question.

'How did you make the bunnies?'

'**Ur-urk!**' I said. About time

someone asked that rather interesting question.
How indeed? Cudweed was only too happy to
tell us.

'Well,' he said, happily. 'It's very easy; all
you do is get the hat, and say "Wugga-wugga-
ding!" over it, and out pops another bunny.'

Solstice considered this.

'And the hamster and the duck?'

'That's three questions already,' Cudweed pointed out, 'and you've threatened me with a fourth. Anyway, to start with, I couldn't remember exactly what the magician said. So my first few tries were a bit off. First I tried "Wigga-wigga-dong!" and got Mr Whiskers, and then I tried—'

'Wait!' cried Solstice, 'Don't keep saying all these things or there'll be even more animals to clean up after!'

'Oh, no,' said Cudweed, 'That's okay. Because I don't have the hat any more.'

'And where is it now?'

'Four,' said Cudweed.

'Four what?' asked Solstice.

'Questions, of course. Four already. I don't have the hat any more, because I have lost it.'

'Lost! Where?'

'Five. If I knew that, it wouldn't be lost, would it?' Cudweed said, with a great and terrible logic.

'Well, where did you last have it?'

'Six. In here. I haven't seen it since . . . well, since the last time I saw Fellah.'

Solstice groaned. I said the rudest thing I have possibly ever said.

'Garrark-rurk!'

'And you don't think that those two things might possibly be connected?' Solstice asked, on the verge of losing her patience with Cudweed entirely.

'Possibly. Does that count as a question or not?'

'Never mind that,' Solstice wailed. 'Here's my second …'

She stopped and corrected herself.

'Here's my *final* question for you. And I would like a full and utterly clear explanation by way of an answer.'

She looked very stern indeed, and even though I'm a brave bird I was a tiny bit scared myself as Solstice glared at her brother.

'Okay,' said Cudweed in a very small voice indeed.

'What on earth are you going to do with all these rabbits?'

Fourteen

When no one's looking, the stable boys have a favourite game; they sneak into the castle and slide down the polished floor of the Long Gallery. Whoever isn't caught and beaten by Nanny Lumber wins.

I suppose I've seen more than my share of weirdness over the years at Castle Otherhand, and things weren't exactly normal in the days of the Deffreeques. There's a titchy clue in their name, after all.

But never, in all my years as castle raven, despite the dangerous, odd, spooky, strange, scary and otherwise momentous events that have happened here, never has there been an event quite as *fluffy* as this one.

Solstice's question about what Cudweed was going to do about the rabbits was a good one, and despite the fact that she had put in a plea for a very good answer, what Cudweed actually said was fairly brief.

'I don't know.'

Then he dashed over to the window to stop a fight between Mason and Tuck Tuck, or was it Nibble and Cagney? I forget, but I'll be blowed if I'm going to get caught up in the whole bunny name thing.

But if we thought the bunnies in Cudweed's room was the start and the end to the matter, we were very much mistaken.

However, I'm getting distracted by the thought of all that white furriness.

Solstice left Cudweed's room, telling him to think about what he'd done. If this was supposed to make him think that maybe what he'd done was not a good thing, I suspect it had the opposite effect. As we shut the door I'm sure I heard him chuckling.

Over lunch we were treated to more excuses
from Madame Zozo about why she was still
unable to read Minty's fortune, and Minty
seemed to have no idea that she might be being
taken for a ride. I made up my mind there and
then that I was going to expose this obvious
fraudster, or my name isn't Edgar Otherhand.

Actually it isn't; Otherhand is only
my adopted surname, and my middle names
. . . well, there's no way I'm going to tell you
my middle names. My parents had a sense of
humour, let's just leave it at that.

'Honestly, Edgar,' Solstice said after lunch as
we wandered through the castle, 'I don't think

Cudweed knows quite how much trouble he'll

be in when he gets found out. And he will

get found out, sooner or later. Did you see

all that white rabbit hair on his jumper? It's

only a question of time, and in the meanwhile,

well . . . What's he going to feed them on? And the smell! It's bad enough now, but give it two days, and . . .'

She didn't need to finish. It would, I knew, be very whiffy indeed.

'I'm going to see if I can talk some sense into him,' Solstice said. 'Maybe there's a way of making them jump back into the hat and disappear. If only we could find the hat. Coming?'

'**Ur-urk!**' I said. I was not.

'Suit yourself,' Solstice said, 'but if you're thinking of spying on Mother's friend I do wish you would reconsider.'

Well, obviously I ignored all that, and flapped off Solstice's wrist, because I *was* going to spy on Madame Zozo, and in order to do so,

I had to beat her back to her room.

I was halfway there when I heard someone call my name.

'Edgar!'

It sounded like Cudweed.

I stopped mid-flap and flumped heavily onto the carpet in the Green Corridor. I looked about me. No sign of him. Thinking I must be imagining things, I took wing once more and was about to spin around the corner when I heard Cudweed again.

'Edgar! Edgar!'

But once again there was no sign of the chubby chap.

I was convinced I was losing the tracks in my train set, when I remembered the mystery of Valevine's voice from earlier that day. Solstice had heard that too, so I knew that if I *was* going bonkers, I wasn't the only one.

But the voice seemed to have vanished as suddenly as it had come, so I sped along, and soon came to Zozo's door.

I was in luck!

There was a maid in the room, doing a little bed-making. Unseen, I crept in behind her, and stood under the wardrobe while she finished. I didn't have long to wait.

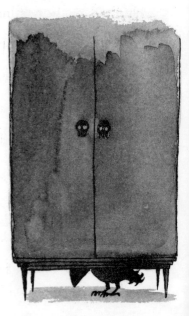

Five minutes later she was off to loaf about in the kitchens, no doubt. She didn't even clear up a tray of tea things that sat on the bedside table. Sloppy work!

She did, however, shut the door behind her. So that was that. I would have to see my plan through now, and wait until either Zozo returned, or the next maid came a-calling.

Just as well I'd had some lunch, because it turned out to be a very long wait. I spent some time rootling through the things on the dressing table, but there was nothing much very interesting. I think I'd been hoping for some rather obvious clue that the fortune-teller was in fact a fortune-hunter, but my hopes were not realised.

After a while I got bored and then I

probably have to confess that I may have had
a teensy-weensy nap, because the next thing I
knew there was a rattle at the door.

Panicking, I looked for a place to hide,
and in a fluster, I flicked the lid off the large and
abandoned teapot on the table, and jumped in,
just as Zozo entered the room.

Unfortunately, it appeared that Madame wasn't much of a tea-drinker, and I found myself up to my waist in cold tea.

This had better be worth the trouble, I thought, but then I panicked again, as Zozo wandered over to the bed, muttering.

'Don't they have maids to do this sort of thing?' and before I knew it, she'd picked up the lid of the teapot and set it back in its place. I ducked inside as far as I could, thinking she must be going to see me, but no sooner was I shut into a small dark and wet space than she was off, muttering about something else the maids should have done.

There was silence for a while, as I sat in near-darkness and great wetness, but then I heard Zozo talking to someone.

Curious, I stood, the lid of the teapot balanced on my head, and risked taking a crafty look at what was going on.

Up periscope!

I was in luck. Madame Zozo had her back to me, but she was talking on a mobile phone.

What she said went roughly like this.

'No. No. She doesn't have a clue. None of them do.'

There was a pause while she listened.

'Mad. The whole lot of them! But no, they have no idea.'

Another pause.

'Don't get shirty with me! I'm doing the best I can. This place is enormous! It could be anywhere! Okay, okay. I know it's what you do best. Tonight then, I'll let you in at the kitchen door! Midnight, yes. And then you can try and find this treasure too. Two heads are better than one. Okay. Now I've got to go. This wig is killing me! No, I told you. I've stood right next to her for hours on end and she hasn't recognised me.

Well it was many years ago, but . . . oi! You

cheeky . . .'

Then she

looked at the phone

as if it was a dog

that had licked her ear.

Clearly, whoever it was

she'd been speaking to

had hung up on her.

So! I'd been

right all along! And

she had some kind of

accomplice too. I didn't understand everything

she'd said, but I had no time to think about

that, as right then she spun around, eyes fixed

on the teapot.

'Time for some more tea, I think!'

I dropped back down inside, and ten minutes later, after a maid had brought a fresh pot, and carried me out in the old one, I was free.

As soon as we were two corridors away, I burst out of the pot, spraying cold tea and clattering cups as I did so, and scaring the poor maid half to death.

But I could not worry about that. I was on to something, and now I had to think of a way to expose our fake fortune-teller!

Fifteen

Edgar once managed to stay in the air for two days, even sleeping on the wing. He had no idea why he did it, and afterwards his wings ached so much he couldn't fly for a week.

'**I** am simply the greatest genius ever to have stalked the Earth!'

It was Valevine, and he was looking exceptionally pleased with himself.

It seemed that he had finally perfected his cabbage-counting machine, and had had Flinch carry it down to the landing of the Small Hall, where he insisted everyone gather for a demonstration.

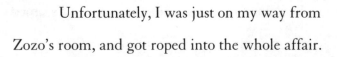

Unfortunately, I was just on my way from Zozo's room, and got roped into the whole affair.

'Ah! Edgar!' declared Lord Otherhand. 'How grand to see you. You are, as always, a good omen in this old homestead of ours. Even if you do seem to smell of . . . what's that . . . Earl Grey?'

He was in an unusually good mood.
I struggled to remember the last time he'd been
so friendly.

'Why don't you sit yourself down on
the bust of Deffreeque there, and you'll have a
wonderful view? There's a good raven.'

I did as I was told. Below me, on the
chairs that Valevine had set out, sat the rest of
the family; Minty, Solstice, Cudweed, Grandma,
Cook, and a few other serving staff. The twins
rolled about on a polar bearskin rug, and seemed
to be the only ones not about to have their
afternoon wasted.

'Isn't your new best friend coming?'
Valevine asked Minty, a touch sarcastically.

Minty snooted.

'She has to have a lie-down after lunch, in order to become better attuned to the universe.'

'Better attuned to the universe . . . ?' Valevine drawled. 'What utter clap-trap! Never mind, the rest of you can marvel at the mechanical magic which you are about to witness. Flinch! Prepare the machine!'

Now Valevine has made some peculiar looking devices in his time, but this one quite took the monkey.

There was a chute, and a hopper, and a funnel, and pipe, and a trapdoor, and then there were about a dozen things which I don't know the name of. But all in all it looked as if someone had bred a combine harvester with a lawn-mower,

and possibly added a dash of snooker table, and
this was the result.

Flinch did as he was told, and bent to the task of winding a starting handle at the side of the machine. After a few violent tugs, the thing sprang into life, and began slowly trundling sideways across the floor of the landing.

'Flinch!' roared Valevine. 'Belay that machine! It seeks to be off!'

Flinch found some bungee cords from somewhere hidden about his person, and used them to secure the machine, which now lurched and tugged like an angry tiger.

'Is that . . . er . . . thing . . . quite safe?' Minty enquired from the chairs below.

'As houses!' cried Valevine, which was none too reassuring given how lethal the Otherhand household can frequently be, especially to kitchen maids.

Valevine stepped forward.

'And now, you shall be the first living beings, excluding Flinch and myself, to witness the cabbage-counter in action! Flinch! Prepare the cabbages.'

Now this was the part that was worrying me. All the cabbages that had run amok in the cellar, and a few more besides, hung in a large net above the hopper of the machine. At a conservative guess there were a few hundred of the green monsters hanging there, ready to be counted.

'Flinch!' roared Valevine, but then he winked

and dropped his voice to a whisper to issue his final instruction: 'Let's count cabbages!'

Flinch tugged at the drawstring of the net and, a moment later, the first cabbages were dropping into the hopper and disappearing into the bowels of the machine, which received them like a hungry dragon.

There was a rumble and a thump, and then suddenly, a large display popped out of the side of the machine, bearing the number 'one', and at that moment, the first cabbage popped out of the front of the machine,

and rolled amicably down the staircase.

'It appears to work,' Solstice said to Cudweed, and indeed it did.

The cabbage landed gently on the Small Hall floor, and Fizz and Buzz looked at it, and then one of them, and it might have been Fizz or it might have been Buzz, said, 'One'.

The next cabbage was already on its way and the machine's display changed from a 'one' to a 'two'; all seemed to be going well.

The second cabbage plopped onto the polar bear and Fizz and Buzz pointed.

'One,' they said.

Now, I think it was about the time that the third cabbage arrived, slightly faster than before, that I began to sense danger in the air.

'One,' said the twins.

And by the time the fifth one arrived, having been spat out of the front of the machine at such speed that it hit the far wall of the Hall, people began to run for cover.

Except for the twins.

'One,' they said, pointing.

Before we knew what was happening, cabbages were being shot out of the counting pipe like smelly green cannonballs, and the Small Hall was no longer a safe place to be. People were dodging and weaving as tattered leaves rained down, and cabbage hearts splattered over priceless paintings and antiques.

'Flinch!' roared Valevine. 'Shut it off! Shut it off!'

Flinch wrestled with the big lever on its side, but the beast had got stuck. Flinch began to kick the thing.

And it was then, as I hopped off my perch to avoid a particularly wide shot from the counting machine, that I saw my first bunny.

When I say 'first', I am not referring to the ones I had seen earlier in Cudweed's room, but to the ones that were suddenly appearing from every doorway and crevice in the Small Hall.

The first bunny began to speed through the cabbages, adding to the total mayhem, and it's really remarkable how fast a rabbit can shift when it's got a mind to. And suddenly, where there had been just one rabbit, there were dozens of them. People shrieked, bad words were said, and cabbages and bunnies mixed freely.

'Flinch!' Valevine shouted again,
'Turn the blasted thing off! Off, I say!'

Flinch was by now whacking the machine
over the head with a mace he'd borrowed from
a nearby suit of armour, and the machine was
responding by spitting cabbages out at an even
greater rate, and with even greater venom.

Bunny, cabbage, cabbage, bunny.

It was hard to know where to look, so I
didn't. I tucked my beak under my wing, and
flew blind out of the Small Hall, and didn't
stop flying until I was sure that both rabbits and
vegetables were well behind me.

Sixteen

The northern side
of the castle is
covered in ivy
so thick and
heavy that around
four thousand
starlings have
made it home.
The noise when
they're roosting is
ear-splitting.

It was a hard afternoon, and the castle had, to be honest, gone to pot. Valevine stomped back up to the laboratory, dragging his machine behind him like a reluctant cow.

Loud banging and thumping, drilling and sawing was heard all across the Great Court as he tried to fix the problem with the cabbage-counter. So that was one less thing to worry about; but there remained the issue of rabbits.

They were everywhere, and though we hadn't actually counted them, it seemed pretty obvious that there were more than three hundred and forty-three.

'Cudweed!' cried Solstice, 'Have you let your bunnies out?'

Minty waded over through cabbage leaves and rabbits.

'No!' wailed Cudweed. 'They're all still in my room. I don't know where these are from! I don't!'

Minty towered over Cudweed.

'It sounds like you have some explaining to do, young man,' she said sternly.

Cudweed trembled.

'I have some new pets,' he said, 'just one or two.'

Solstice nearly exploded.

'One or two! Cudweed!'

So then the whole thing came out, and Minty marched Cudweed up to his room so he could show her his 'one or two' new pets. No sooner had he opened the door, however, than there was a mass breakout, and every single rabbit burst out of his room and down the corridor, eager to join the fun with the other bunnies.

They left behind two other creatures.

'Who,' said Minty, 'are they?'

'That's Mr Whiskers,' Cudweed

explained. 'And that's Mucky Duck.'

'And who is Mucky Duck?' asked Minty, foolishly.

'Oh,' said Cudweed. 'He's just a duck.'

'And you say you don't have the magician's hat any more?'

Cudweed shook his head.

'And Fellah hasn't been seen either,' Solstice added. 'You can bet that monkey has something to do with it.'

'Perhaps,' said Minty, 'but that doesn't explain where all the rabbits are coming from. In order for the hat to make a rabbit, you have to say the magic word, yes? What was it, wugga-wugga-ding? Yes, so even if Fellah has the hat, he can't be making the rabbits because the last time I checked, Fellah was unable to speak.'

Solstice looked at her brother.

'Cudweed,' she said, 'You didn't produce anything else from the hat, did you? When you were trying to remember the right words for bunnies?'

Cudweed went a very funny colour then, and it appeared that he had realised something. Something bad.

'Well,' he said, 'there was Mr Whiskers. And Mucky Duck.'

'Quack!' said Mucky Duck.

'Quiet, Mucky Duck!' Solstice said.

'And then . . .'

'Yes?' asked Minty, even more sternly.

'Then there was this funny sort of bird . . .'

'Yes?'

'This funny sort of bird. He looked a bit like Edgar, but he was smaller, and had a yellow beak, and . . .'

'Yes?!'

'And he could . . . um . . . talk. Sort of.'

There was silence for a moment, then Minty made a funny sound in her throat. I thought she might faint.

'Are you trying to tell me that you made a mynah bird?'

'What's that, Mother?' asked Solstice, but I could have told her. Mynah birds are funny little things who, though I hate to admit it, do have a certain skill that ravens do not. They can talk. At least, they can mimic the human voice. And very realistic they can be, too.

'And did you, by any chance, still have this mynah bird in your room when you were saying "wugga-wugga-ding"? At all?'

Cudweed went purple.

It all became clear.

The disembodied voices calling to Solstice, and to me.

The rabbits coming from nowhere.

Somewhere in the castle, there was a small black bird sitting on the edge of a magician's

hat, repeatedly saying 'wugga-wugga-ding',
probably with an amused monkey watching a
continuous stream of rabbits jump out of it.

Seventeen

Edgar's longest
ever sulk was a
record-breaking
four weeks, at the
end of which he
finally relented
when Solstice
offered him
twenty-three
dried mice and
a honey toasted
sandwich.

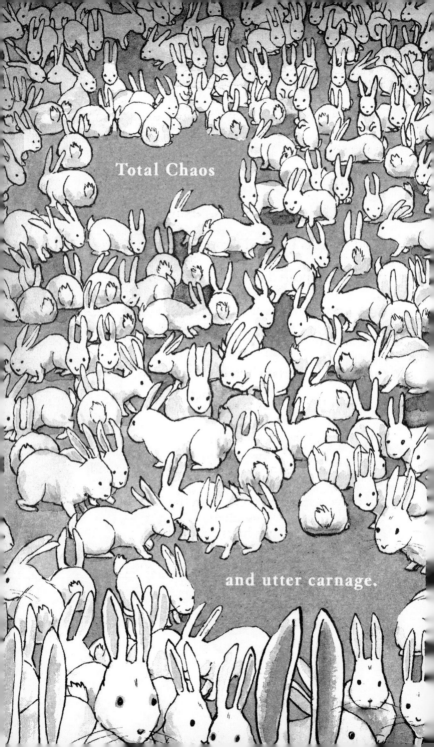

At six o'clock that evening I took refuge in the sky, as it was the only place free of little cotton fluffy tails.

They were appearing at an increasingly rapid rate. As I looked down from high above, the castle appeared to be infested with white fluff. Great carpets of bunnies were scampering here and there, doing all the cute bunny things that cute bunnies do but, let me tell you, when they number in their thousands, it becomes very much less cute.

Valevine and his machine had reappeared, but he was sent scurrying from the Hall as a gang of delinquent rabbits charged at him, hopping into the machine and out of the pipe at the bottom.

Suddenly every rabbit in the castle wanted to do the same thing. It was like a fairground ride for them, and you could almost see the smiles on their faces as they sped out of the counting tube.

Strangely enough, the machine appeared to have begun to work properly, and I watched with horror as over the next half hour the counter on the side crept up into the low tens of thousands.

'Mother!' wailed Solstice. 'We have to do something! Can't you use some magic?'

Minty looked rather unsure.

'Well, it's been a while, you know.'

'Mother!'

'Very well,' Minty said. 'First of all we need to find the hat, and stop any more rabbits coming out.'

But actually, in the end, it was yours truly who put a stop to the rabbit production, aided by Cudweed.

'Would it help if we knew where the

mynah bird was?' he asked, suddenly showing a degree of sense.

'Very much so,' said Minty.

'Oh, good,' Cudweed said. 'Because he's sitting on the top of that statue of the third Lord Otherhand.'

'Well, why didn't you say so?' screamed Minty.

'But I did,' said Cudweed to Solstice, sounding rather hurt.

I didn't hang around to hear any more, and sped towards my smaller bird cousin at a terrifying speed.

'**Rark!**' I cried; the blasted bird had seen me coming, and shot off the statue as if in some sort of Olympic event. Undaunted, I pursued, and there followed a dramatic high-speed aerial

chase through the length and breadth of the castle.

Now, I don't want to go into too much

detail here, but I have to concede that the pesky

little bird was fast. Very fast. I could barely keep up.

The chase took on a new dimension as we twisted and turned through a series of chimneys and hidden passages, and then back into daylight. Still I was not gaining on the mynah bird, but finally, finally, the young bird began to slow, and before too much longer I was able to peck him on the backside, which was enough to send him scurrying for cover.

And cover turned out to be the trunk room in the Grey Attic, where I found Fellah too, staring into the magician's top hat, unable to work out why no more bunnies were coming out of it.

'Wugga-wugga-ding! Wugga-wugga-ding!' cried the mynah bird as soon as he saw the hat again, and two rabbits appeared, as if by magic, which, I suppose, it was.

Fellah shrieked with delight, but I took my chance and snatched up the hat in both claws, and sped like a slippery rocket back towards the Great Hall, where I found Solstice, Minty and Cudweed, backed into a corner by about four thousand rabbits.

Letting the hat drop into the safety of Minty's hands, I squawked so loudly I scared a narrow path through the bunnies, allowing the family to make their escape.

'Go to your rooms!' cried Minty, clutching the hat for dear life. 'Everyone! And tomorrow we'll work out what to do about these blasted babbits. I mean runnies! I mean . . . oh, never mind. Just run!'

And we did.

Eighteen

Valevine has always
been obsessed with
the way things
work; his greatest
achievement as a
boy was dismantling
his father's car.
Sadly, although he
managed to put
it back together,
it never quite
worked again.

Midnight approached.

The Otherhands were resting, whereas I was hard at work!

My holy mission to save the castle from filthy thieves was soon to be underway.

I prepared for battle. Mostly by eating my way through a small pile of dried mice, followed by a little chocolate mousse. I do like a little sweetness after rank decay. And mouse and mousse, what's an extra 's' between friends, anyway?

I had not forgotten Madame Zozo's mysterious phone call, and her plans to meet her even more mysterious accomplice at the back kitchen door.

I pondered awhile on the lot of the raven, and the great burdens that are placed at my feet on occasion, but then I thought another dried mouse might cheer me up, and it did. Somewhere, deep in the depths of the castle, I heard the clocks strike midnight.

It was time to act!

I left the Red Room and, although I'd been locked in my cage, they still haven't worked out how I flick that little section of brass bars to let myself out, so off I went, as stealthily as only an old raven can.

The castle was silent, but eerie.

And full of rabbits. But they were quiet now; the little bunnies were tuckered out after scampering through the cabbage-counter all afternoon, and were sleeping it off, dreaming about carrots and such like, I suppose.

I took great pains to glide as noiselessly as I could above the resting rabbits, because I didn't want a repeat of the chaos we'd seen earlier that day. Not yet, anyway. They carpeted every corridor and hallway like the deepest fluffiest sheepskin, or even rabbitskin, rug you've ever seen. Though slightly smellier.

Quietly I headed for the kitchens, and yes! There was my foe.

Zozo, or whoever she was really, tiptoeing very, very carefully among the rabbits.

I sat on the end of the spit roast as she crept towards the back door, and turned the big

key in the lock, being very careful not to wake a single rabbit. She let her accomplice in.

If Solstice had been there, she would have gasped.

For there, sneaking in, was a thin and nervy-looking figure who I recognised instantly as the grumpy ticket collector from the circus!

That was enough for me!

I zoomed towards them, in the devil of a bad mood, and, having given the ticket man two quick pecks on his skull, I lunged at Zozo, and plucked that wig right off her head!

I was away.

'Stop that bird!' cried Zozo, but they were no match for my speed, especially when the floor was knee-deep in bunnies.

They followed me out into the dining hall, and immediately stumbled into approximately fourteen thousand rabbits.

Now, I don't know if you've ever heard the sound a rabbit makes? It's not much to speak of, if I'm honest, a small snuffle and the occasional squeak, that's about it. But if you multiply that small squeak by about fourteen thousand, you suddenly get rather a loud noise indeed.

So I put the final part of my plan into action, and circled round the room, letting the pair of robbers try to catch me, but never actually letting them do it.

Five minutes was all it took to wake the whole house and have everyone come charging down, where they found . . .

One raven, a duck, a hamster, a mynah bird, a monkey and several thousand bunny-wunnies. Oh, and two robbers.

'Gasp!' said Solstice, as she recognised the ticket collector. 'It's the ticket collector.'

Smart girl, I thought.

'Do you mind?' snapped the robber, rather

grumpily. 'I'm no ticket collector. I'm Pete the
Thief, known to police throughout the country
as Sneaky Pete.'

He seemed to be rather proud of that.

'Madame Zozo!' cried Solstice, 'What are
you doing with Sneaky Pete?'

And then there was a surprise, because
Minty had suddenly spotted something, or rather,
someone, without her wig.

'Goodness!' she declared. 'That's not
possible. Is it you? You!'

She screamed at
this point.

'You! It is you!
A little fatter and much
older! But you!'

'Why, you—' began Zozo, but Minty interrupted her.

'This is not Madame Zozo at all, but my arch enemy from Witch School. I haven't seen her in years, but ... oh yes, I see it now. Even uglier than before, is that nose real? Why, yes! It's my old adversary, Helena Handcart!'

The atmosphere was thick.

The floor was covered in bunnies.

And we were all about to see just how wild things can get when two witches go mental.

Nineteen

There are parts of the castle that are so long-forgotten that no one knows what happens there. And there are some pretty strange beasts lurking in the cellars of the Lost South Wing, just waiting to come out and play . . .

Helena Handcart sneered at Minty.

'You!' she cried. 'Who are you calling old? Look in a mirror some time!'

Minty nearly fainted, but recovered herself enough to hurl some more insults back.

'And,' she added, when she'd done with that, 'Just what do you think you're up to in my home?'

'I would have thought that was obvious. We've come to steal the fabulous lost treasure of Otherhand. You always were the best at witch school, weren't you? You were the prettiest, your spells were the best. I hated you for that! And then you married the richest man in the country. I know you're sitting on that loot somewhere . . . Now hand it over!'

'Gasp,' said Solstice, again. 'Edgar, you were right all along.'

'**Ark!**' I cried. Thank you very much. About time.

'And Sneaky Pete is your accomplice, is he?' Valevine asked, a little slow on the uptake.

'Yeah,' drawled Pete. 'Now hand over the loot, old geezer.'

That was too much for Valevine.

'For one thing,' he said, 'the word is "yes", and for another thing, I am not a "geezer", and for a third thing, we don't know where the treasure is ourselves. And for a final thing, even if we did, do you think we'd just hand it over to the likes of you and your crumby friend here?' Hah! I think not!'

'Well said, husband,' stated Minty, proudly.

'Actually,' Helena Handcart bawled, 'I think you might just hand it over, especially when I've finished with you! Try this for size!'

That's when the fun and games really started.

Helena Handcart began waving her hands about and muttering some strange words, rather like the wugga-wugga-ding thing, but longer.

Suddenly she fizzed something through the air at Minty, who all of a sudden was covered in snow.

'Is that the best you can do?' Minty cried and, thinking hard, waved her hands about and sent something magic back at Handcart, who suddenly found herself standing in a bowl of soup.

'Oh, bother,' said Minty, 'I knew I was out of practice, but really!'

Handcart sneered.

Another spell winged its way across the room, and would have struck Minty full in the face, but she ducked, which was good. What was less good was that the spell hit a maid standing behind her, who was turned into a piglet.

The piglet oinked sadly, but otherwise looked none the worse.

'Why, you—!' cried Minty. 'Very well, you asked for it! Prepare to die!'

She waved her hands a bit more, and mumbled something in Greek, and a moment later, there were a host of butterflies sitting on Handcart's head.

'Blast,' said Minty. 'They were supposed to be tigers.'

'Oh, please. Make them stop,' Handcart said, very sarcastically. 'Enough messing around. Prepare to die, yourself, Euphemia Otherhand!'

Another spell, but Minty was ready, and cast a protecting spell of her own, which sent Handcart's bouncing off in a wild direction, smack into Sneaky Pete's nose, which

immediately turned into a carrot.

'Ow!' said Sneaky Pete,

holding his nose. 'Dad hurds!'

One or two of the

bunnies began to eye his

nose hungrily.

'Right!' Minty

announced. 'That's it!

No mercy!'

And with all the energy

she could muster, she sent her

very worst spell at Helena Handcart.

Well, there was some effect at least, this

time, as Helena Handcart instantly turned bright

green from head to toe.

'Oh,' said Minty. 'I really am out of practice.'

Handcart laughed and sneered, and sneered and laughed.

'Right,' she said. 'Now hand over the loot, or I'll turn you all into badgers.'

About then, I had the inkling of an idea. It might just work, but it would need Solstice's help, and quickly!

What I had remembered was this: the spell that Solstice had tried to teach herself from Minty's old spell book. How to make rabbits hate greens . . .

Could it work?

I wasn't sure, but I had to get Solstice to think my way and, to do that, I began pecking the nearest bunny like I'd never pecked any bunny ever before.

I went completely doolally.

Solstice saw me, but would she understand?

'Edgar,' she said, 'Not now. Why are you pecking that rabbit, anyway?'

I pecked some more.

'Rabbit?' Solstice said.

 Futhork! Hurry, girl!

Work it out!

I could see that Handcart, although green from head to foot, was about to unleash something terrible on us all.

'Edgar!"
Solstice cried. 'Yes!'

Now she began to wave her hands about, mumbling something about rabbits, and a second later, she cast her spell on each and every bunny in the room.

Handcart, whose attention was on Minty, didn't see the end coming. One minute she was all evil witch, doing evil witchy things, and the next she was attacked by somewhere over fourteen thousand rabbits, who had all suddenly decided that they really didn't like greens, greenery, or anything green at all . . .

I won't describe what happened next in great detail, but it's probably enough to understand that even a nibble can become lethal when multiplied by enough sets of chompers.

Sneaky Pete fled, a couple of rabbits dangling off his carrot nose. He went screaming down the drive and that was the last we saw of him.

'Good heavens!' cried Valevine. 'What an absurdly bizarre night!'

Solstice laughed.

'True,' she said, 'But Edgar saved the day. What a clever raven you are!'

'Rark!' I declared, because Solstice had played her part too.

And after that, there remained one question.

'So,' said Valevine, 'what . . . er . . . what are we going to do about all these rabbits?'

And it wasn't just the rabbits.

There was also a hamster, a mynah bird, a piglet and . . .

'Quack!'

'What in blazes is that?' barked Valevine, spinning around to see a small fowl standing behind him.

'Quack!'

'Oh, him,' said Cudweed. 'That's Mucky Duck.'

'And who on earth is Mucky Duck?'

'Oh,' said everyone at once, 'he's just
a duck.'

Well, that was the end of the excitement with
the cabbages and the bunnies, and if I'd wanted
something to stave off my boredom, I certainly
got it. All in all, it was a little too much for me,
but as I tucked my beak under my wing that
night, I realised something.

It was time for the two-week absence I
take from the castle every twelve years. I would
have to leave in the morning, and go off on
the secret and mysterious leave known to all as
Edgar's holiday . . .

Little did I know what a fatal time it

would be to leave the castle, and all its crazy

inhabitants, unattended.

Postscript

The question of the bunnies was soon solved.
A couple of days after Sneaky Pete and Helena
Handcart had sneaked into the castle, the
magician from the circus came calling. The
presence of several thousand bunnies cannot
be kept secret for long, and word had spread.
Taking his hat back from Minty, and arching
one eyebrow, he merely said 'ding-ding-wugga',
and each and every bunny vanished, on the
spot, never to be seen again. Although I'm sure
I've seen some white tails flicking through the
woods recently . . .

The Raven Mysteries

Is my beak wonky? Am I going grey? At the very least I suspect I may have fleas again.

But no matter, I, Edgar, Guardian of the Castle, long-standing protector of the endlessly stupid Otherhand family, and fine example of ravens everywhere, am proud to present this most wonderful piece of modern technology.
Not another useless invention from his Lordship, I hear you ask? No, this actually works.

To find out more about The Raven Mysteries books, read my blog, explore the Castle, meet the family, search for the lost treasure of Otherhand, and much more, visit . . .

www.ravenmysteries.co.uk

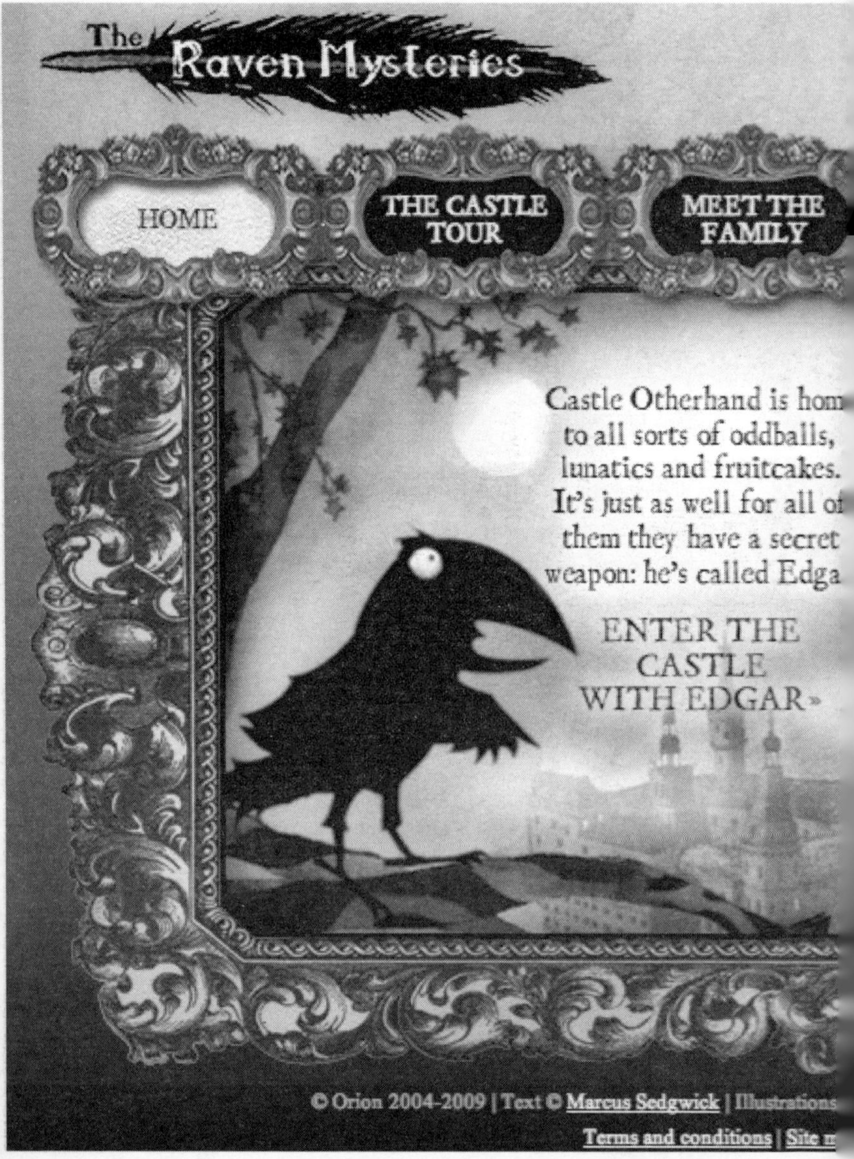

The Raven Mysteries
HOME
THE CASTLE TOUR
MEET THE FAMILY
Castle Otherhand is hom
to all sorts of oddballs,
lunatics and fruitcakes.
It's just as well for all o
them they have a secret
weapon: he's called Edga
ENTER THE CASTLE WITH EDGAR »
© Orion 2004-2009 | Text © Marcus Sedgwick | Illustrations
Terms and conditions | Site m

th-Froth Members Entry Gate: LOG-IN / REGISTER

TURN SOUND ON

BOOKS AND AUDIO

GOTH-FROTH

AUTHOR & EVENTS

VISIT THE CASTLE CLASSROOM!

GO

LATEST BOOK 'LUNATICS AND LUCK'

FIND OUT MORE

ELLAH 'S EDGAR GAME or registered Goth-Froth fans only!

LOG-IN TO PLAY

LUNATICS AND LUCK

son | Music © Peter Rinne | Site design by HyperlaunchDMG

Goth-Froths on Facebook

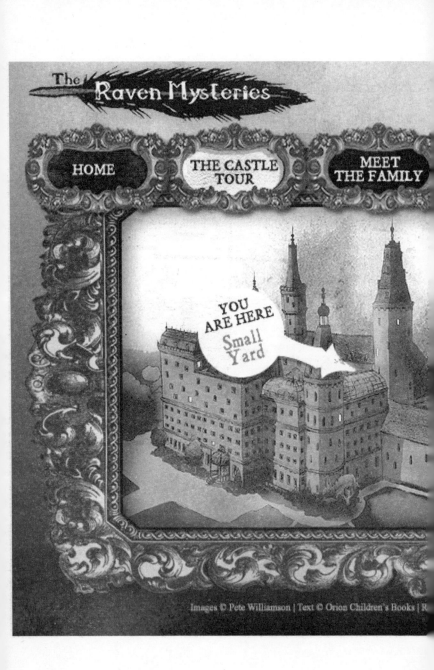

oth Froth Members
Entry Gate:

EMAIL

LOG-IN

THE
BOOKS

Otherhand
Castle

☠ GAME

♥ PRIZES

ᔕ DOWNLOADS

Chapel

Other
Courtyard

Great
Hall

Ballroom

YOU
ARE HERE
Small
Yard

Small

Great
Courtyard

Small
Yard

Dining
Hall

East
Tower

Gardens

Kitchens

N

W — E

S

Stables

CLOSE MAP